Laurence kissed his wife's head. He then slid a hand under Michael's head. The baby slept on.

" 'Begin, auspicious boy, to cast about thy infant eyes and with a smile thy mother single out. Thy mother well deserves this—' "

He stopped abruptly, his mouth drying, his limbs cold.

" 'Thy mother well deserves this short delight.' That *is* how it continues, is it not?"

Lavinia stroked Laurence's cheek. Tears streaked under her touch.

"Oh, my love, take heart. Virgil was not writing our tale. Whatever comes, this bit of humanity is a miracle. Our miracle . . ."

"The world of eighteenth century Scotland, with its reason-filled university life and its outer islands where crofter magic still works, is beautifully evoked in this elegant, elegiac fantasy novel."
            —Jane Yolen, author of *Tales of Wonder*

Other fantasy titles available from
Ace Science Fiction and Fantasy

Daughter of the Bright Moon, Lynn Abbey
Ariel: A Book of the Change, Steven R. Boyett
Jhereg, Steven Brust
The Broken Citadel and *Castledown*, Joyce Ballou Gregorian
Idylls of the Queen, Phyllis Ann Karr
Songs From the Drowned Lands, Eileen Kernaghan
The Riddle of the Wren, Charles de Lint
Harpy's Flight and *The Windsingers*, Megan Lindholm
The Door in the Hedge, Robin McKinley
Runes of the Lyre, Ardath Mayhar
The "Witch World" Series, Andre Norton
Tomoe Gozen, Jessica Amanda Salmonson
The Revenants, Sheri S. Tepper
The Seven Towers, Patricia C. Wrede
Sorcerer's Legacy, Janny Wurts

and many more!

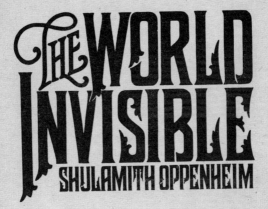

THE WORLD INVISIBLE

SHULAMITH OPPENHEIM

ACE FANTASY BOOKS
NEW YORK

For Gabrielle

THE WORLD INVISIBLE

An Ace Fantasy Book/published by arrangement with
the author

PRINTING HISTORY
Ace Original/August 1984

ISBN: 0-441-91018-1

Ace Fantasy Books are published by The Berkley Publishing Group,
200 Madison Avenue, New York, New York 10016.
PRINTED IN THE UNITED STATES OF AMERICA

This is love: to fly towards a secret sky,
to cause a hundred veils to fall each moment.
First to let go of life.
Finally, to take a step without feet.
To regard this world as invisible,
and to disregard what appears to the self.
Heart, I said, what a gift it has been
to enter this circle of lovers,
to see beyond seeing itself,
to reach and feel within the breast.
My soul, where does this breathing exist?
Bird of the soul, speak in your own words
and I will understand. . . .

Jalaluddin Rumi   *circa 1244*

Prologue

On a warm October day only a few years past the middle of
the eighteenth century a boy was born on Unst, the most
northerly isle of Shetland. He was named Michael Magnus,
laird of Burrafirth. His father, Laurence Bruce, gave the
title to his son immediately. It was good, he said, for the
boy to grow up knowing who he was and what such a rank
entailed.

The child came into the world under the same canopy as
had his father and his father's father and those before him.
The first laird had sailed from Norway in the fifteenth century. Acquiring land from the Scottish throne he settled in
the north of Unst, ruling a domain above a line running east
to west from Haroldswick to Flubbersgerdie.

The four years of marriage before Michael's birth seemed
an endless waiting for the parents. To them his appearance
was near miraculous.

Laurence rocked the infant close against his chest.

" 'Sicilian muse, begin a loftier strain. The lovely boy
with his auspicious face' . . .'' He smiled at his wife
propped up by a mountain of linen pillows sweet with
herbs. "I can't help thinking of the fourth eclogue of Virgil,
where he speaks of the birth of Salonius. Do you remember,

Lavinia, we read it together shortly after our marriage, translated by Mr. John Dryden?''

Lavinia turned her head to the window. She could see the firth, Burrafirth, her firth. The water's surface was barely catching the dawn, throwing it back onto the sky. She was usually alone, swimming, by this hour, she and the firth, the two of them welcoming the dawn. Now there would be three.

"I remember, my darling.'' Lavinia held out her hand and Laurence sat down on the side of the bed, laying their son between them.

" 'The knotted oaks shall showers of honey weep.' '' Her voice was husky with the fatigue of childbirth. Laurence heard it and put a finger to her lips.

" 'The fates when they this happy web have spun shall bless the sacred clue and bid it safely run.' ''

"Laurence, his life will be blessed, will it not?''

Laurence kissed his wife's head. The curls, like springy heather, were damp along her brow and down her cheeks. He slid a hand under Michael's head. The baby slept on.

" 'Begin, auspicious boy, to cast about thy infant eyes and with a smile thy mother single out. Thy mother well deserves this—' ''

He stopped abruptly, his mouth drying suddenly, his limbs cold.

" 'Thy mother well deserves this short delight.' That *is* how it continues, is it not?''

Laurence dropped his head onto her breast. The baby squirmed and uttered a thin cry.

Lavinia stroked his cheek. Tears streaked under her touch.

"Oh, my love, take heart. Virgil was not writing our tale. Whatever comes, this bit of humanity is a miracle. Our miracle.''

Chapter One _____

WHEN MICHAEL WAS five, his mother died. She was found on a flat rock on the far side of Hermaness, near Humla Stack, shielded and warmed by the seals. She never opened her eyes or spoke for the three days before her heart stopped beating. How she died, of what she died, no one could say. Laurence buried her in the cemetery high above Bluemull Sound. As the peaty earth held her body, Laurence held his grief within him, and as Michael grew more and more like his mother in face and spirit this grief, rather than easing, swelled with the unshed tears. More and more the father withdrew from too frequent encounters with his son.

Michael ran free. Days would pass, the two would not meet. Only at night, candle in hand, would Laurence stand over his child, allowing the pain some release. The old nurse Anny watched over the daily needs of the boy, her own grief and fears unspoken. Finally in the spring of Michael's ninth year she broke her silence.

"Master Laurie." Anny handed Laurence the evening tea, then clasped her hands behind her back. "Master Laurie, I cannot do it. The laddie is needin' more. Ye've been givin', but it's more he's needin'. It's time."

And so Laurence decided to entrust Michael's formal

education to a tutor. Rather than choose the man by letter, he journeyed to King's College, Aberdeen, the site of his own education. At the home of a friend, in the great reception hall, he interviewed those interested in the post. Finally he called back Robert John, twenty-five years old, a young man with a wide and deep knowledge of Latin and Greek, French and Hebrew, mathematics and logic, physics and metaphysics. The course at King's College was still set up on the medieval system with Aristotelian logic at its base and a strong emphasis on languages. It was however the system of regenting—one teacher carrying the student through the whole curriculum—that appealed to Laurence. He knew the regent had to be a walking encyclopedia, precisely what was needed for a boy with a quick if undisciplined mind on an isolated bit of earth far to the north of the great universities and centers of intellectual activity.

Robert John stood in the doorway. During his first interview all his mental faculties had been directed toward his questioner. Now the room's beauty struck him, the elaborately stuccoed ceiling, the marble fireplace massive and carved, the walls covered with the finest arras. Laurence was pouring claret from a pewter stoup. Two more contrasting figures would be hard to find. The Shetlander stood tall, uncommonly so, with white hair straight back from a high, bony forehead. His steel-blue eyes were set deep under black brows. The Scot was of medium height and slightly more than medium weight, with russet hair cut to meet a trimmed beard framing a wide face. His long nose stood resolutely between heavy-lidded hazel eyes.

Laurence motioned Robert into the room. Handing him a glass, he indicated a chair by the window and sat down opposite him.

"Now," he began, then drained his goblet, "a question. It has no bearing on anything other than my interest in you as a person as well as a scholar. Why do you wish to leave King's College and Aberdeen?"

"With your permission, I prefer not to answer, sir," was the reply so immediate as to give Laurence the distinct impression that Robert had anticipated the question. This reply was accompanied by a slight blanching of the young man's cheeks and an almost imperceptible tightening at one corner of his mouth.

"Fair enough. I'll begin then with a description. Our manor sits by the head of Burrafirth on what is called the Ness. Grey stucco, rather somber I'd say, compared to an Aberdeen residence." He smiled and both men looked at the mantel and the hearth with its huge brass andirons on which a mammoth log blazed and crackled.

"It *is* well heated, however, the weather being cruel more months than less. We've an extensive library. And an extensive staff." The man peered at Robert. "You're not one of those against keeping servants, are you?" Not waiting for a reply he volunteered, "If you are, let me tell you I released my tenants years ago. All have been born on the estate, as have their parents and back for generations. Nurse Anny came into service when she was fifteen, the year I was born. I am now"—he rose and went over to the wine table—"I am now fifty. Too old to raise alone an unruly colt of nearly ten."

Refilling his goblet, Laurence raised it to the light.

"Wine-dark. Homer was always to the mark, but the seas around Shetland are leek-green."

Laurence walked slowly back to his chair. Robert sipped the liquid. It was warm but it cooled his throat.

"Your time, how you spend it, is your own. I would like my son civilized as well as cultured. Right now his edges, perhaps even his interiors, are rough, though he knows well the ways of a gentleman. We are *not* the barbarians depicted by Westminster and even, if I may say so, hereabouts. And"—he drew in a long breath—"we are not as isolated as is believed. There are visitors from abroad—not often, but still they come—and the mail arrives quite regularly, again not often by city standards, but with its own regularity."

The color had flooded back into Robert's face. He felt it spreading across his forehead and along his ears. He seized upon the last sentence.

"I'm not that much for socializing. I'll be happy to spend my time with your son." He paused. "Sir, I must tell you. It is true I applied for the post of tutor with great hope of success. But I know as well as do you, you might choose between far more experienced, distinguished minds than mine."

Laurence waved a protesting hand and again finished off the wine at one draught.

"Don't underestimate yourself. You have much scholarship. And more. It is for this 'more,' as well as for your intellect, that I have decided. Till now, the boy has been raised by myself and Anny. My wife, as I told you when we first met, died four years ago. She drowned." Laurence's voice dropped and his eyes looked beyond Robert, beyond the walls of the room. "She was an excellent swimmer; we called her the water sprite. She spent as much time in the firth as out, yet is it to be believed, she drowned." He ran a thin, long hand through his hair. His eyes were half-shut. "Where was I? Yes, raised by both of us, but most of

Michael's time has been spent with the crofters, the fishermen, and the servants. Especially Anny. You can imagine"—and here the hand was raised in a cautionary gesture—"he has been instructed in and protected by every charm existing; his head has been filled with the tales and superstitions in which Shetland abounds. His imagination has been enough fed. The time may be overdue to stimulate his mind. Though it *is* true"—and again the eyes searched beyond their listener—"our minds reveal a natural tendency to assimilate one thing to another, to think rationally. So, perhaps—" Laurence smiled. "Perhaps he has more in his head than I credit him with."

Robert gave a worried tug at his beard. The gesture was not lost on Laurence.

"Speak up, Robert John." Laurence leaned back and crossed his legs. "I've no doubt you've given the subject some thought. It's in the air, you might say. What is reality, what are merely appearances of reality."

"In thinking, I myself am not against stimulating the imagination along with the mind. One without the other . . ." He hesitated and balanced his feet against the chair legs. "Imagination alone imparts to perception a form other than the original, could you not say, bringing about a new idea. So—one without the other . . ."

"Yes?"

"I cannot see, thinking on the question, how products of the mind are worth a whit without the imagination. Take Ovid." Laurence nodded. "Ovid is filled with reflections to which only the imagination has access, a hidden world. . . ."

" '*In nova fert animus mutatas dicere formas corpora.*' " The words came slowly from Laurence, as if he were reach-

7

ing back, pulling them from out of that very hidden world of which they sang. "'My intention is to tell of bodies changed to different forms.'"

Laurence raised both hands, then let them drop onto his lap. "I agree." His voice was suddenly tired. "I agree, but I cannot fully describe what must be tempered in my son's nature until you have seen our island. The moors are a melancholy mystical sight. The valleys—straths, we call them—are lonely as a cleft in the heart. The cliffs, stupendous; the foam surges. All tend to dreaming away from the real world and its pain. Yet life *is* harsh, is it not?" He stopped, stood up, and began filling his glass for the third time, Robert's for the second. "I shan't bore you. You shall see for yourself. It is an elemental world, stripped of all pretense. Utter loneliness forces man back into himself, which can be . . ."

"Good *or* bad." Robert finished the thought, his own voice distant, removed.

"You understand." Laurence smiled a slow, wry smile, full of a past that Robert suddenly felt, with regret, might be forever closed to him, the newcomer from Aberdeen. Then unexpectedly the older man laughed.

"I, too, was once drawn to that hidden world, desiring a lifetime roaming the moors with the sheep and birds and my shelty as my sole companions. So I know how far one can be drawn and how hard it is to return. The truth is . . ." Laurence walked to the window, pushing aside the heavy damask curtains. "The truth is, I cannot educate the boy alone. My wife left us just when—" He swung around still hanging on to the damask. "I told you she drowned? We *think* she drowned. We found her with the seals." His knuckles were white around the stem of his glass. "Asleep with the seals. Is this rational? Is this reasonable? The answer is no, but you see, in the final analysis I am a Shetlander and I must protect my son. . . . Enough!'' He started for the door.

Robert set his glass down beside the stoup.

''With your help Michael shall see the world as it is.''

Robert stood up.

''For the last time, sir, I am *not* all reason myself. Are you sure it is I whom am best suited to teach your son?''

Putting out a hand in farewell, Laurence looked into Robert's face.

''I am,'' he answered simply.

Chapter Two _____

ROBERT WALKED SLOWLY along King Street toward the flat
he would be quitting in two months. It was final. They had
shaken hands on it.

Cold for June. He drew his cloak about him.

He could tap out this route blindfolded, he had walked it
that often. Was he blindfolded now? What path was he
tapping out for himself? As a teacher he could be relentless.
Recently he had become relentless with himself. What path
indeed. He was the only child of a father who had been a
noted barrister in Aberdeen and a mother renowned for her
learning and sweetness. A tranquil childhood had been their
legacy to him. Now both were dead, ten years dead, and he
had attached himself to . . .

Robert did not have to shut his eyes to see her as he had
for the first time. Bright-faced, hair the color of broom
falling about her cheeks and neck, pearls the size of cher-
rystones in her earlobes. He had been lured to a detested
"soirée" by a friend under the pretext of viewing a play, a
rare event in Aberdeen. He recalled, protesting, "Alexander, this is not the way to the theater." His friend and
colleague had taken firm hold of his arm. "Stop fretting like
a pregnant cow and come along!"

Nearly ten years older than Robert, he was known as
Alexander the Great, inspiring a strong allegiance without
deep affection. In Robert, as in others, Alexander inspired
something else, a morbid stirring far less accessible. From
his eyes, veiled yet glittering, came the warning: I make the
overtures of friendship. I decide when there is to be inti-
macy and when there is to be distance. Despite moments of
unease, the arrangement suited Robert. He had no desire to
become familiar with anyone.

Or so he had thought, before that evening.

Alexander pulled him through the door of a seven-storied
house in Clubber's Close, where he was instantly divested
of his cloak by a servant, who swung his arms limply like
the wings of a dead bird. Alexander was crooning under his
breath.

"Look immediately to your left, O prudent scholar. That
mare is Isobel, daughter of Lord Henry and Lady Susanna
of Eglinton. Would you believe, there's not a buck in Aberdeen would not throw down the glove for her sake!"

At that moment Isobel turned. Her smile was as bright as
her eyes.

"Why is that surprising?" Robert felt his chest tighten.

Alexander swung his friend toward the supper table.
"God's breath, man, *déjà* smitten!"

It was a sign of a leisurely attack, Robert had learned,
this peppering the conversation with French.

"You look astounded. Here, have a glass. I'll warrant
you've not come near this quality nectar before, impecunious scholar that you are. Here." He lifted Robert's hand
and stuck a bubbled stem between his fingers.

"I'll tell you why it's astounding, this rush for the young
Isobel. For she is just out of the schoolroom, so to speak."

Alexander was already refilling his glass, his tone half-admiring, half-satirical.

"Because she's inordinately intelligent, old fellow. A thoroughbred—rich, elegant, and educated to the nines. Geography and logic and natural theology. Her father's a madman!"

He bent over his friend.

"But then, truth to tell, we're all after her, hearty comrades who would make the ultimate sacrifice. To wed in order to bed! How must it be, O wise one, to make love to a woman with more in her head than feathers? Do you think it affects one's vital member, hardening it beyond one's wildest hopes, causing it to cut through the soft, moist barrier with thrusts more powerful than the whaler's harpoon?"

He should have left then and there. Instead he left Alexander draining a third glass, and wandered about on the edges of small gatherings, unfamiliar faces, never completely out of sight of Isobel. After making three turns about the room he suddenly found himself face-to-face with the young woman. The hand she extended was finely shaped, slim, the nails rosy.

"You're Robert John, Alexander's prudent scholar. And you wish you were a thousand miles away, am I right? I'm Isobel Eglinton and I, too, would be transported, by whatever means!"

That was it. Just enough time for him to notice the pale-brown mole by the corner of her underlip; the small, rounded set of her teeth; the almost brazen twinkle in her eyes when she spoke. A moment later she was spirited away from him by one of the young bucks and within minutes Robert, too, was gone.

He locked his door to everyone except his students. To

Alexander the door opened a crack. "Stay away, *s'il vous plaît!*" was written in flourishing script on a paper thrust into his friend's hand. The last time he had so secluded himself was after his mother's death. He was lovesick and he knew it. What he absolutely did not know was what to do about it.

After seven days the painful quandary came to an end. A note from Isobel arrived asking him to meet her by the old bridge of Balgownie. How had she known it was his most preferred spot in the city, with its Gothic arch and surrounding foliage? It was there as a child that his mother had taken him on golden summer afternoons. There he'd spent hours leaning over the arch peering into the dark salmon pool below. It was to this bridge that they had walked, he at fifteen, just after his father had died. It turned out to be the last walk together before his mother's death a few days later, a death never explained by doctor or minister. Robert brushed a sleeve across his eyes, remembering. Without a word she had slipped away into the dark salmon pool. Oh, well he understood his new employer when Laurence had spoken of Lavinia's bewildering demise and his own incredulity. And now, after nine years, a young woman with hair like the sun, fair as his mother's was dark, was calling him to that exact spot to tell him:

"It is you I desire, Robert John. You, not the empty-headed, vapid, roistering bucks that fawn and slobber. Yes, I am bold, but with you there is no other way, is there? Will you have me?"

Robert hurried along King Street. Yes, he would have had her but her father would not have him. He had not been *enough* for the Lord and Lady Eliot of Eglinton. He had not passed the one examination of his twenty-five years in which he burned to shine. How could he? He couldn't do an about-face for the great lord. He was, precisely, Alexander's prudent scholar—no more, no less. He was doing exactly what pleased him. And doing it well. Educating young minds—young minds whose judgments on him, however harsh, could not wound, for they were only judgments, not privations. If he *was* prudent, it was as much by choice as by nature. Who could know when a beloved friend just might disappear, slip away as his mother had done? Who could chart the many dark pools along the journey? Better to move cautiously.

And so he had. Until Isobel. Why, he might have followed his father into the law, but the law meant visibility. Barristers must be seen as well as heard. Seen and heard! Robert gave a sharp, angry laugh. He had been seen all right, but not heard, that infamous afternoon. Only a week ago. After meeting secretly in obscure tearooms, wooded parks on the outskirts of the city, and by the bridge of Balgownie, Isobel decided it was time he met her parents.

"Come for refection, at four o'clock tomorrow," Isobel said. "It's time you met my parents."

Robert caught up her hands and kissed their palms.

"Time they met me, isn't that more to the point? Is it not to tell them we are in love, and to receive their blessing?"

How clear the next moment! Isobel moved away from him and leaned over the bridge. White daisies and black-eyed Susans fringed the banks of the river on either side. A pair of ducks hovered in and around the reeds while their offspring made sport under the water. Swinging around, she spread her arms along the smooth stone ledge.

"We *are* in love, sweetheart, but . . ." Isobel extended her hand. The lace cuff fell across her fingertips. "Robert, my father is a stern man, afraid of no one. He was raised to power and admires the powerful like himself. He . . .''

Robert moved to embrace Isobel but stopped abruptly. In an instant her words put an end to the idyll of the past month.

''He'll have little use for me, is that what you're saying? Little use for the scholar who has had the audacity to fall in love with his treasure? Well then, let's have done with it!''

His voice was reaching an ugly pitch, but right then he cared not a whit for his voice, for the Eliots of Eglinton, for—

''Robert, stop! Hear me.''

''I hear you, Isobel. I only wish you had warned me before. Oh, my love, you know I cannot fight a man such as your father! You knew from the beginning, which is why, now that I think of it, you have taken a month to speak of our meeting. If he will not have me as a son-in-law, then . . .''

''Then *what*, Robert John?''

So he met with her father. Lord Eglinton had made it quite clear that a ''struggling'' teacher, no matter how respectable his family, was unacceptable as a husband for his daughter and father for his grandchildren. He had then retired to a corner with his lilliputian teacup lost in his great pawlike hand, and remained silent. Robert had raised Lady Eglinton's fingers to his lips, bowed to Isobel, tipped his head to the lord, and left.

He had not answered Isobel's notes that followed—five, sometimes six a day, left under the door by her footman. No, instead he had answered the notice: ''Tutor desired to intelligent child, nine years old. All subjects required.

Commencing in August. At Burrafirth, on the island of Unst, Shetland. Those who wish to apply, kindly leave credentials with the Office of the Chancellor.''

Shetland. Ultima Thule, the early Roman explorers had called it. In his mind Robert had traveled the world, but he'd never been to Shetland, a two-day trip from Aberdeen. Tacitus had written that when Agricola had sent his fleet to coast around the northern portion of Great Britain after the battle of Mons Grampius in 89 A.D. they had sighted Shetland. Robert's heart skipped. Now he would sight this same land, set foot upon it, enter the home of strangers and make it his own for however long he was needed . . . and wanted.

Robert slowed his pace and a man walking close on his heels fell against him.

''What *was* the name of that Irish priest who had commented on Shetland?'' Robert spoke directly to the unfortunate, who was picking himself up from the ground and dusting off his hat. Bits of molding vegetable leaf clung to his cheek and mud, full of stench and flies, dripped from his pant leg as he scurried away, muttering maledictions just loud enough to be understood by his assailant.

''Diciul was his name,'' Robert called after him. ''My apologies, good man.''

Robert quickened his step. That monk Diciul had written that a certain other honest monk one summer had visited islands in the northern seas after sailing from Ireland a night and a day in a two-benched boat.

''Well, well.'' Robert kicked a glob of refuse. ''Here prepares another monk to sail.''

He turned the corner into a narrow wynd and down six stone steps to his door.

"I have taken the decision." He pulled the key from deep within his cloak pocket.

"It is I who have decided." He placed the metal into the lock.

"It is *I*." And Robert felt a surge of energy fill him, the first since he had hastened from Eglinton Manor and his beloved, vowing never to see her again.

The dank, narrow stairway, worn and sloping, was free of traffic. In this building lived a barrister, a dancing master, a clerk, a lord of the session, an ancient countess who wore her tiara to bed, and a shopkeeper whose sign, a butter firkin, banged through the night on its rusty hinge just outside the front window.

Robert John would miss them all, and he found himself smiling at a specific memory, of the barrister's account of a trip to London where he was surprised to discover that the higher up in the building one lived the cheaper the rent.

"So I said to the landlord, I ken weel what gentility is, sir, and after living ma life in a sixth story I amna come to London to live on the ground."

Yes, he would miss them. As alien to one another as their personalities and backgrounds had been, they had managed to live together in harmony. Robert glanced down at the stone steps. It was not usual for so traveled a staircase to be kept as respectable as this one. But all the residents agreed on a modicum of cleanliness. Pooling a few pounds a year, they employed a sweeper who came twice daily, swept and emptied the luggies in which was deposited the filth.

Robert loosened the collar of his cloak. One slow flight up. Two more months of it. Was Shetland clean? Islands had to be cleaner than— The door in front of him, to his flat, was ajar. The servant girl? She had already been and gone, early that morning.

There was a decided scent in the hallway. Only one did he know who smelled of tuberose. Isobel. He hadn't noticed her horse. . . .

She was standing by the bookcase, a small, thick volume open in her hands. Her outfit was completely free from the restraints of high fashion. In place of the wide hoops in which women maneuvered like ducks, a solid-tone mauve silk gown fell loosely from a high neck, outlining her full breasts and hips. Her hair was without powder, the unruly waves and curls framing her face. A six-strand choker of pearls lay glowing against her pale skin, her color heightened by her errand. The only concession to current mode were her slippers with three-inch heels designed to aid the wearer in stepping over the garbage of street and stair.

Her voice stopped him in the doorway.

"'But something else was needed, a finer being, more capable of mind, a sage, a ruler. So man was born, it may be, in God's image. . . .'" Isobel paused and placed the book carefully back into its space. "I want to hear the next line from you, Robert, from your lips. Please."

The cold in his hands had overtaken his whole body. As a young boy that passage had been his introduction to Ovid. Had she somehow divined it, or had a ribbon marking the pages guided her? Marking the page, yes, but he had not marked that particular verse.

"'All other animals look downward. Man alone, erect, can raise his face towards heaven.'"

Isobel pulled off her gloves and sat down. Her smile was

as soft as her voice, but there was a trembling of her bottom lip.

"Quite a challenge for man, don't you think, my love? Ovid had imagination. He knew what was required of man to live fully. Risk! You know. Why then—"

Robert moved into the room, slamming the door behind him.

"Why then did I not act the man, when your father, who is *not* God in Heaven, passed judgment on me without a shred of evidence save my shabby cloak and scholar's hands?" He advanced on Isobel, his palms turned upward, fingers spread wide. "Inked, Isobel of Eglinton, inked like the printer's press. Was this your father's dread? That I might defile his rose of Sharon, his lily of the valley? That there lurks the passionate tendencies of a Moor beneath this cloak? That in the night I turn black as, as . . ."

"I'm not here to apologize for my father. You know me well enough. If his behavior was inconcinnate, he must answer for it. I am concerned only with us, with your reaction to him as it affects *us*." She pulled at a long strand of hair by her neck, a gesture Robert had come to both love and fear because it spoke of pain contained, anger rising. "There *is* still an entity known as *us*, is there not? For me, beyond a shade of doubt. I cannot believe, therefore—"

"I leave for Shetland in two months." Robert swung off his cloak and laid it over a trunk by the fireplace. "I am now tutor to the young laird of Burrafirth, who will be ten years old in October. An only child, motherless. We shook hands on it, his father and I. An hour ago. Done."

"Done!" Isobel was up, the gloves hanging between her fingers like a flail. Her cheeks were bright-red. "Done! Challenge you and you run, is that it? What did you want?

My father wishes to marry me off to a rich boor, despite my own education. I wish to marry you. You wish to marry me. Fight, then! Fight, for God's sake and for our own!''

"I want him to accept me as I am and give us his blessing. Is this too much?''

"Yes, it is. *It is.*'' She slapped her arm with the gloves, the words a furious whisper. "Far too much for my father. But is his not having done so enough to destroy what is ours *by right of love?* You are right; my father is *not* God, neither here on earth nor near Heaven. So why buckle under? *Why,* my love, when it comes to it, buckle under to God or my father, or to *anyone,* Robert. Why?''

The shrill cry of the fishmonger was her only answer. Robert dropped into a chair opposite Isobel. Her upper lip was beaded with sweat. Why did he feel a morbid satisfaction? Was it her turn to sweat? An elegant mare, chafing at the bit—for the first time, he'd wager.

After minutes he spoke.

"I have no explanation.''

"But you're gloating, that's clear.'' Isobel got up. "I'll tell you what I think, whether or not you wish to hear it. You're a petulant coward. Oh, you love me. But you've been wallowing in self-pity for years, under the guise of— what does Alexander call you?—the prudent scholar. Along comes my father, determined, *over*determined, with his raw pride, and you are so angered by his strength that you cower and creep away. Yes, that is what you are doing. Creeping north. I can only pray that you are put to some kind of test in that part of the world. The crags and cliffs are also raw; harsh storms and tempests mark the winter months, making their own demands. You're surprised? Yes, I've been there. My parents love those islands, clean, clear, untouched, majestic. What a bizarre turn, that you creep north to a world which has always been presented to me as God showing himself at his most wondrous and inventive. Birds, seals . . ." Her hand was on the door pull. "Go there. It will do you no end of good, if you are more open to its challenges than you have shown yourself open to the challenges of love. Go and—" Robert was about to speak, but Isobel put a finger to her own lips.

"No. Leave it now. As you say, it is done. Go and godspeed."

The sound of her heels on the stone punctuated the air. Then, like smoke dispersed, it was gone. She had left her gloves behind.

Chapter Three _____

MICHAEL STOOD IN the middle of a thick patch of seapinks, a pony by his side. The two had reached the end of Hermaness after a long climb and trot. The going had been slow, because the bonxies, the great skuas of Shetland, were everywhere, guarding their eggs laid in hollows of umber-colored earth, exposed to the equal danger of weather and predator.

"Stand still, Jaimie," Michael instructed the pony as a bird swooped toward them. It came directly for their eyes, then, with a shriek, it veered up and away.

"Father says to stand *very* still. They're protecting their babies that are coming." The beast pushed its muzzle against the boy. Jaimie was a beautiful animal. His mane was thick and black, his body—like his master's—slim and sturdy, the color of a golden plover's breast. Michael responded to the pony's touch by putting a thin arm about its neck and drawing it close.

"Anny said to me this morning, 'Da spring is i' da eart.' She's right, Jaimie. It's been here but we haven't seen it, with all the rain. Look at the pinks! Let's go to the *very* end."

The heather was dry and brown, but in between the

prickly low-lying plants, spotted orchids were pushing up to the sun and the bird's-foot trefoil gave a dashing display of yellow where the pinks left them to their own. The song of the lark was full and watery. Holding fast to the leather rein, Michael led the way around the tiny pools that dotted the moor, reflecting sky and cloud. Soon they came to the end of the promontory jutting out into the sea.

They were well over six hundred feet above the water. Directly in front rose the rocky Muckle Flugga, the last bit of English soil. Far below to the left the seals lay sunning and sleeping. Every few minutes the water was broken by one emerging, to clamber onto a space made free by a companion who decided to cool off with a graceful plunge. A puffin lumbered out from a hole in the ground, its broad beak a triangle of bright-orange. The air was filled with the cries of gannets and guillemots and gulls circling and circling, then coming to rest on the nesting ledges of vertical cliffs.

Michael drew in his breath.

"Jaimie, *look!* There must be thousands of birds. Father should come. He *should*."

He found himself a safe spot, not too close to the edge but near enough to watch the seals. The pony stayed placidly nearby.

"I'm to have a tutor, Jaimie." Michael drew up his legs and rested his chin on his knees. His dark hair fell in loose curls over his head, in front almost to his eyes, which were sky-blue like his father's but slivered with golden flecks.

"Do you suppose we'll have time to ride together?"

Jaimie gazed at him.

"I really don't know why I'm to have a tutor. I know how to read, English and Latin. I can read all of Father's

24

plant books in Latin; he taught me long ago. And I can recognize all the plants and birds when I see them. And I can row and use a tuskar to help cast the peat blocks—" He hesitated. "A little tuskar! And I've driven the sheep and helped with the shearing. I don't think I need a tutor, do you?"

The pony lowered its head as if in agreement. The air was suddenly clear of birds, their cries stilled. And up from the water came a new sound, high, thin, and sweet.

"Jaimie!" Michael was whispering now. "Jaimie, it's the seals! Hear! I know what they're singing. 'Michael doesn't need a tutor.' Suppose this tutor doesn't like seals and sheep and climbing down into caves for a baby lamb that lost its footing. Suppose . . ."

Michael stood and buried his face in the animal's mane. In a moment the fur was wet with tears. Jaimie didn't stir. The puffin took courage and waddled closer. A lamb bleated across the headland and Michael could not stop the weeping. For minutes his frame shook with grief. Then he breathed deeply and wiped his eyes and face on his tunic sleeve.

"Come on, Jaimie," he said, pulling at the rein. "Anny will be looking out for us. Come on."

The pony snorted and turned southeast to walk a diagonal line across the moor toward firth and home.

Anny was at the door. Her face, wrinkled as a walnut shell, was pinched as she ran up to the pony and swung Michael down from his perch.

"What! It's more'n half a day we've been lookin' fur ye. Ye always say!"

She hugged him against her. She smelled of peat smoke and mutton and spring.

"We went to Hermaness, Anny. All the way. I wasn't alone. Jaimie was with me and Murphy came partway."

Murphy, called sheepdog but of dubious origin, opened one eye as he lay by the stoop in the sun.

"Aye," Anny countered, "Murphy came partway but when he was back and no laddie, what was there to think? Eh? What?"

Then relief overcame her and she gave a loud cackle of laughter. "Ye be back and that's the matter ended. Come in and have a warm bannock with milk, to hold ye until supper."

Michael's mouth was full of oatcake as he dangled his legs from a high wooden stool in the large kitchen. The fire had been rested, covered over, for the June air was warm, but it could be stirred to life at any moment. Anny stood at a table in the middle of the room chopping cabbage into fine shreds.

"When will Father be back?"

"Don't be talkin' with food in the mouth. And drink the milk."

She laid down the knife.

"Tomorrow, weather allowin'. At least, so was the plan. But ye can never know. Olaf might be here with a letter sayin' it's all changed."

"And I'm really and truly to have a tutor?"

Michael looked up over his mug as a thin line of milk dripped down his chin.

"Aye, ye must be a fine gentleman, with fine manners and learnin'. Ye might even be *talkin'* Latin this time next year."

She came over and ruffled the boy's head.

"But mind ye, don't forget the tongue ye be born with. I wouldn't want to be learnin' the priest's tongue, not now."

Michael laughed and the drip became a flood.

"I'll always talk to you, Anny. But . . ." He gulped down the rest of the milk, biting hard on his lower lip. "I don't know if I'll like him. My tutor."

"Ye'll be likin' him." Anny took the cup and set it down by a pitcher on the sideboard. "Yur father is not one fur choosin' a body ye might not take to. We'll all like him." Anny had long taken it on herself to speak for the other servants. The last was said with a conviction not quite free of threat toward those who just might feel otherwise. *"We'll all like him."*

Michael rubbed his thighs.

"Jaimie's broadening out. I'm stretched, Anny."

"Give us a look."

Anny bent over Michael's legs, pushing here and there from the ankles, past the bony knees scarred from scrapes and falls, up to the firm brown thighs.

"It's muscles all right. Tight they are. Tonight we'll rub in a pad o' sheep's fat and ye'll drink a cup o' tormentil tea. It's fur all the griefs."

Then she took up her knife and started slicing again.

"What if he doesn't like it here? He won't have mansions lit up with thousands and thousands of candles and lords and ladies dressed in jewels and silk and . . ."

Anny put down the knife once again, wiped her hands on a cloth that hung from her belt along with a ring of keys, and took Michael by the hand. She sat down in a wide chair by the hearth and pulled him onto her lap.

"Look here, laddie. Ye be makin' yurself sick over this

tutor. I doubt yur father be choosin' one who puts stock in such goin's-on.''

Michael would not be put off.

''There's the weather, Anny. What about the weather? The wind. And it's dark most of the day in winter. And all my friends. Ivar and Olaf and the crofters and fishermen. He won't understand them.''

Anny was rocking back and forth, Michael close to her bosom.

''Ye be bound to see him gone already, and him not even set foot on Unst. He'll learn. He'll be quick, I'll warrant.''

They sat quietly.

''Anny.'' Michael sat up and put a hand to the woman's cheek. ''Do you think he'll *care?*''

''Care? About ye? Why else would he be comin', laddie?''

The boy shook his head.

''Not for me. For Murphy and Jaimie and the birds and you and''—he whispered the word—''the firth. Will he care about the firth, and the seals, and the magic? Will he?''

Anny pushed back Michael's hair. ''Aye, ye be one fur worryin'. And at such an age. Don't ye be thinkin', he knows we're an island. He's probably comin' first off fur ye, then fur bein' with water all 'round, mark me. Stop frettin', laddie. He'll be fine, just fine.''

Michael lay back against her warm, full body. There were other smells now—spray and salt and turned earth. He lifted up his head.

''Did you know my grandfather, Anny, Mother's father?'' he asked, pointing to a large painting on the wall in front of them. It was a trial portrait for another hanging in the parlor. He added shyly, ''My gudsyr.''

The head was of a young man with waves of titian hair framing his face. The chin was wide and firm, clefted, and the eyes an exact match with the younger ones looking at them. Not only the eyes, but every feature save the color of the hair, was repeated in Michael's face.

Anny knew the face well. She gazed at it a moment, then back to the child in her arms.

"No, he'd passed away when yur mother was a young girl, but lookin' at you, he's here now. He'd be one to follow. It was him founded a home fur the blind, in Edinburgh. Never was such a thin' before. No place fur the poor creatures to go and most families not wantin' to keep 'em."

"My grandfather was a doctor, wasn't he?"

Anny's mouth was suddenly a straight line.

"That's somethin' else. That's fur city folk, them that don't know the real ways o' healin'."

"*Anny!*" Michael put a finger to her lips. "Anny, it was a doctor set my arm when I broke it."

"'Twas yur father's thought, that. We've charms enough fur healin'. 'Twas the charm healed it, fur all the bits o' wood the doctor tied 'round it." She caressed the boy's left arm, which was wrapped about her neck.

"And I'll croon ye the toothache song, just to remind ye." She grinned, her own mouth naked of teeth.

> "A Finn came ow'r Norroway
> Fir to pit tooh-ace away.
> Oot o' da fleash and oot o' da bane.
> Oot o' da sinew and oot o' da stane.
> And dare may do remain.
> And dare may do remain.
> And dare may do remain."

She opened her eyes. Michael's head was on her shoulder and his eyes were shut. She lifted up his head and set him on his feet on the floor, pulled her skirts about her, and got up.

"It must be nearin' fi' hur. . . ." A hand flew to her mouth. "Ye have me speakin' the old tongue. It'll be suppertime afore we know it. Get up to the basin and wash the milk from yur face. There's a bit crusted about the chin. And scrub those hands. Jaimie may have his ways but he's also got fleas and earwigs and heaven knows what else, I'll warrant."

Michael ran up two short flights to the landing where a table stood with an ample white washbowl and matching water pitcher. The open window looked out on the firth. A lark's trill bounced off pink clouds. The surface of the water was like a thin covering of shattered glass, and opposite, the rocky wall of Saxavord was almost black.

"My firth." Michael leaned out of the window. As a lover speaks of his beloved he echoed himself.

"My firth."

Chapter Four _____

LAURENCE RETURNED WITHIN the week. It was a placid
two-day sailing from Aberdeen to Lerwick. There, in Lerwick harbor, he was met by the *Erne*, a slim Norwegian
yawl with a high carved white-tailed eagle, from which it
took its name, set on the bow. The boat was his, skippered
by Olaf Haroldson, an old friend and former tenant whose
family had been fishermen for the lairds of Burrafirth since
the sixteenth century.

The *Erne* was graceful, with a large lugsail on one
slender mast rising up midship. This day the seals were out
in number and the gulls followed the boat as it picked up
wind and glided northward toward Unst.

"Robert John is a fine man, Olaf; sturdy, intelligent, with
a good heart. He'll do, I've no doubt."

Olaf drew long puffs on his wide-bowled pipe.

"Why does he quit his college?"

Laurence smiled. "I asked him that very question. He
preferred not to answer. Each man has a right to his privacy,
so I inquired no further. But at twenty-five, why would a
young man with all to the good about him be leaving? A
soured love, I'll wager. And you?"

Olaf nodded. "Aye, Shetland is about as far as ye can run

when ye've a mind not to run *that far away.*" He raised eyebrows like tufts of dried heather. "Aye, gone but not *quite*, I'd say."

"You're a shrewd one." Laurence settled back on the floor of the boat as Olaf rose, hand on the tiller, the better to maneuver a safe course around a baa, those hazardous rocks hidden at full tide. Seventy years living more on the water than off had given Olaf unsurpassed knowledge of these dangers.

"As to Michael Magnus, he'll not be likin' the harness, will he, master?"

"He'll not like it, but he must begin formal studies and I'm not inclined to send him from home, not yet. It's been long enough, Olaf. Five years have slipped away like a herring through the hand since you carried her coffin, with me half-crazed beside it, to Bluemull. It will be excellent for both of them. Michael will be more than a handful for Robert John, and if a love gone awry *is* the reason for his flight, nothing will be better for him than a half-tamed colt. What news of Burrafirth?"

Laurence turned his face to the sun, the first warm rays of June making his skin tingle. He pushed the broad brim of his hat away from his forehead and loosed the clasp of his cloak.

"Thomas Matheson, he's the news, though it's the same thing, only this time . . ."

"Only this time"—Laurence pulled himself onto the bench that had been supporting his neck—"this time something more ugly, cruel, has happened, what? They say youth is cruel, reckless." He gave a short, angry laugh. "I'd say the old can be far more brutal. They have years to refine their inclinations. Well, let's hear it."

The *Erne* was now safely past the Noup and would soon be entering Burrafirth. To pass along this body of water in silence was always Laurence's desire, but Olaf had a story to tell and it was best he knew the details before arriving home. Thomas Matheson was a cragman who lived alone in a cottage just above the beach at the far end of Burrafirth. He was expert at rescuing lambs (and children) who, gamboling about uncertain terrain, had the misfortune to fall, clinging to the rugged cliffs or dropping onto a patch of sand, or worse, dashed on the sharp rocks cutting the water's surface. This was his "Christian side," as he put it. This same intrepid nature sent him, with equal expertise, to robbing the nests of birds indiscriminately, and finally to dismembering them, also for no apparent reason.

"This year"—Olaf hung on the words—"aye, this year whilst you were gone, he ascended the cliff to the erne's nest, the one near four hundred feet above the sea, on the northwest side of Unst, but he found only two eggs, he tells. You know, Master Laurence, the erne is always about laying three eggs, one of which is barren." Olaf winked, not so much at Laurence as at the idea of such a ruse. "Aye, he took the two, going back a few days later expecting to find, he boomed out to the crowd, the other ready and waitin' for him. 'Well,' says he"—and Olaf warmed to the telling— " 'I see the bird, the female, broodin' in the nest. I sees it by its white tail. I'm creepin' along the shelf o' the rock,' says he, 'till I'm close on the aerie, and I throw my body over the jut o' rock and seize the bird by the leg. It bein' a female, she made no more resistance than a hen or goose, fool that she was. So, undoin' my gaters I tie up the bill and feet, twist the wings one 'round the other, and there she lies, gagged and foolish.' "

Olaf turned to Laurence, his face flushed with emotion.

"He was grinnin' all the while, master, thrillin' to what he'd done, takin' a glorious creature, renderin' it helpless. He's a danger, this Thomas Matheson is; he's to be rid of, he's—"

"Steady, Olaf, we go through this every year. What happened next?"

"What was to be, Master Laurence. Ye know the spot. The only path back be too steep to carry such a burden, so he dropped her and dashed she was on the rocks below. There's no doubt she suffered. Thomas himself recounted she was twitchin' mightily for minutes after and from her tied beak came a sound. Could he not have put her to death before castin' her off?"

"Or let her free when he realized she was too much for him on such a precarious descent." Laurence stood up. "No, Olaf, then we would not be dealing with this particular human being, we would be dealing with a different sort, not Thomas Matheson. I *had* hoped time would gentle him, but it's not to be. He must be near your age, seventy or so?"

"Aye, we were schoolmates together, two of a small band."

Olaf thrust the rudder and the *Erne* cut the water to the right, heading for the stone pier that marked the Ness and home.

"'Twas yur grandfather's idea, bringin' the boys together fur learnin' to read and write. That's what puzzles me. Where's the power o' book learnin' if Thomas couldn't change fur the better? He's a good head on his shoulders, has Thomas Matheson, a good head."

* * *

Behind the house, across a cart path, was a small steading for vegetables and berries. Currants, gooseberries, and strawberries flourished, with rows of the decorative artichoke between. By the left of the manor Laurence had planted a miniature forest of beech and hawthorn, apple and rowan—not only for botanical interest and shade in this treeless land, but in order to attract and give refuge to the small songbirds. Woodpecker and chaffinch, wren and linnet, redstart and fieldfare, all were frequent visitors and many had nested in the wooded oasis.

A few days after his return Laurence stood looking up at a male chaffinch resting on a low bough of an apple tree. Bird and man stared at each other for a moment, but only a moment, for the air was punctured by Michael's hooing as he came hurtling down from the moor, scattering sheep and dogs.

"Slowly," Laurence called to him as Michael tried to retain his momentum on the upward approach to the house and wood. He arrived gasping for breath, smacking into his father, who just managed to catch a clump of earth as it fell from his son's hand.

"A *blue* primrose, Father! I've never seen one but I recognize it. A blue primrose!"

"I don't know how you come by such finds." Laurence smiled broadly at Michael. "It *is* rare, Michael Magnus. You've the botanist's eye and—"

"No, Father!" Michael shook his head vehemently. "Anny says it's because I follow the ferrytuns. The fairies sing, like the seals, only not everyone hears them. Anny says I do. That's how I find all the plants and nests and things."

Laurence put the flower down against a tree trunk, pulled out a square piece of homespun from his pocket, and wiped Michael's face and hands in silence.

"Come," he finally said softly, shaking out the cloth and returning it to his inner vest pocket. "Come into the sun by the front wall. I've wanted to speak with you ever since my return but the days have been full of estate business and the like. This," he added, taking the boy's hand in his own, "this seems to be the moment. Come along."

Michael felt a squeeze about his throat. He would hear it now; it would be true, when his father spoke the words. He had been hoping—he had not asked, but he had been praying—that perhaps his father had not found a tutor who suited. But he knew his father. The grip on his hand told him, the face wiped gently but firmly. The tutor had been chosen.

"Come along," Laurence repeated, and Michael fell into short running steps alongside his father's long strides.

Michael sat cross-legged on the ground in front of his father. Laurence settled himself on a stone bench. A black-backed gull waddled up, eyeing them with tilted head.

"Swaabie's been a *bother,* Father," Michael said, stroking the bird's crown. "He's been following me everywhere. Anny says it's because you're gone and he was watching—"

"This is a perfect example of what I wish to talk to you about, Michael Magnus."

Laurence folded his hands around his knees with the same deliberation he used in choosing his words.

"Anny has been nurse to you from the moment you were born, as she was to me."

It was now Laurence's turn to feel a tightening in his throat as he watched his son's eyes grow suddenly bright. Reaching out, he laid a hand on Michael's shoulder. The boy rubbed his cheek against his father's fingers. The slightest intimation and there were tears. *My God, is there no end to mourning?* Laurence cupped the wet cheek in his hand. *There is no end.*

Neither spoke.

Then Michael said, "Do you know why I love the firth so much, Father?" He shut his eyes, pushing out the last salty drops.

"Why do you love the firth so much?"

"Because Mother loved it. Because when I'm looking at it or near it or in a boat *on* it, I'm near Mother. Besides," Michael added, and his face opened with light, "there is magic under the firth. There are sea spirits and mermaids and mermen and coral houses and crystal streets. Anny told me. All shapes and colors and sizes. That's why Mother loved it." He looked up at Laurence, pleading for agreement.

"Your mother loved what was beautiful. She loved every creature warm to the touch. She loved the island, and . . ." Laurence paused. "It *is* true she loved Burrafirth more than any other place on earth. But," he said, pulling up next to him, "she loved it for what she could see and smell and touch. Which brings us back to Anny."

"And my tutor?" Michael settled onto his father's lap and they sat looking at the water below.

"*And* your tutor. You are right, I have chosen him. His name is Robert John, he is twenty-five years old, and . . . Here now!" Laurence tilted Michael's chin. "Don't look so downtrodden! He is learned and kind and your mother would have felt completely safe putting you in his care. Of this I am convinced.''

Michael nestled against his father's rough tunic.

"Will he let me ride Jaimie?''

"Of course. He will ride with you.'' As he said this, Laurence realized he had not at all inquired into Robert's outdoor accomplishments.

"Will Anny still be my nurse?''

"Anny!'' And Laurence was caught up in another realization. He had no idea how Anny perceived her future role, a factor impossible to ignore. "Yes, Anny *is* your nurse. But I must tell you, there will be far less time for listening to her tales and charms, for gathering herbs and tormentil roots for her teas. You will be busy, reading and studying the works of men who thought a great deal about this world we know, about people and how they act and why they act. They put down their ideas to share with us. It is beholden for us to heed them.'' Laurence pulled at a lock of hair that stood from Michael's head.

"I've read lots already, Father. With you, and by myself. And Anny knows lots about the world,'' Michael countered. "She knows why Breeta's milk turns sour and how to birth lambs and babies and what charms to say when you've a toothache and a headache and—''

"And why that molucca bean hanging around your neck *didn't* turn black when the mist rolled in without warning, keeping you prisoner by the cliff's edge for hours and putting us all in a frenzy.'' Laurence poked at the yellow object the size of a thumbnail and shape of a hazelnut strung along a stout thread.

"I knew to stay still, Father. Anny told me what to do in

a fog. She knows about the world. She said, 'The bean keeps you safe even when it doesn't turn black.'"

"Winning will put a man into courage! Well, well, we'll wait for Robert John. I'll need an ally, I can see it, for it will take the two of us to have any weight against our Anny!" Laurence stood up, with Michael in his arms.

"I love you, and there *is* magic. We'll show you, Father, someday."

Laurence clutched Michael against his chest. His hair was as soft as thistledown. It was sweet-smelling, of the earth and the sea. It was good to hold his son in his arms on a balmy June day, a thing he had not done often enough in these last years. And at the same time the feelings deep within him were bitter and painful, feelings that pierced his heart and drew its blood and filled his mouth with gall.

No magic, no charm kept her with me, brought her back. I held her as I hold you now.

Anny was drawing water from a well in the corner of the kitchen when Laurence tapped lightly on the wall.

"He was that tired, was he, Master Laurie? He's asleep already?"

She put down the bucket and pulled out a chair from beside the table.

"Would ye have time to sit and tell me about the one who's comin'?"

She placed a tray of oatcakes in front of him.

"I noticed ye didn't have one at supper. Ye didn't have much supper, fur all that."

She set a mug beside the tray.

"Ye'll have a drink? The grog is somethin' fine this year."

"I'll drink with thanks, Anny, but I've not come for that." Laurence broke a flat dark cake in half. "Yes, he's asleep."

"When will the one be with us?"

Laurence swallowed the sweet, then drained the mug.

"The one coming is called Robert John, Anny. He'll be with us in August. This gives him the summer to set his affairs in order. And," he added, fixing a steady gaze on Anny's face, "it gives Michael time to become used to the idea."

Anny had been waiting for an opening.

"Fifteen years old I was, Master Laurie, when I took ye up from yur mother's arms, ye with the cord still danglin' from ye. And we never needed another till ye were sent off to Aberdeen." She sat down opposite him. "Mind now, I don't say this to the laddie. I'm tellin' him it's right and proper he has a tutor and takes up studyin', and I'm tellin' him fur all his worryin' his father would not be choosin' an unkind man . . . would ye, master?"

The woman put a hand across the table. Laurence took it in his own. The veins showed deep aqua through reddened skin but the cast was solid, the fingers long and flexible.

"Aye," Anny said, closing her eyes, "that hand rested on yur brow many times and on the brow of the Lady Lavinia, God bless her."

Laurence came around to Anny. Standing over her, in his full height, it was hard for him to imagine her as a girl of fifteen, daughter of a crofter, holding a baby seconds old that was himself.

"As for my staying at home as a young boy, there were

two, a father *and* a mother, to guide me. Besides yourself, of course! My father was young, with boundless optimism and energy and a strong, loving wife by his side. Anny . . . Anny, I'm fearful. I've *been* fearful these last years. I am fifty years old and alone and the charge of Michael Magnus is heavy on me. It's best what I have done." *And you agreed, early on. You said it was best.*

"But Laurie lad . . . Master Laurie . . ." Anny turned in her chair. "*I'm* here. I've taught the boy; we've all taught him. He's a fine way fur learnin' himself. He knows more about the ways o' this land and water girdlin' it'n those ten times his age."

Laurence wanted to answer that Michael needed more, much more, than those *ways* she had taught him, that there were other wisdoms beside her superstitions and peat-fire tales. But he read in her eyes a fear of loss, along with a devotion that could not be matched. So he merely drew her up and put her hands to his lips.

"Rest easy, Anny."

"Lavinia."

Laurence held the pillow against his chest and stomach. The aroma of pungent herbs was as sharp and fresh as their wedding night. Anny kept the little pink herb sacks full. She tucked them into the pillow casings and under the sheet at the foot of the bed.

"Lavinia, I held Michael in my arms today. I shall do it more often, sweetheart. He's growing so like you. I should be glad? I should. Divine cunning, you'd call it, or magic. Yes, I know, they are the same for you. But for me, it only underlines the loss, heightens my pain. Not always, but . . ."

Sixteen and thirty-six they had been. His father had called him into the study to announce that both families were prepared to overlook the unusual discrepancy in age because it was obvious they were devoted to each other.

How they had laughed together in this very bed over the word *devoted*. If to suck in flesh and drink the texture of skin, the shape and odor of breasts and breath, savor the triangles of puff below the navel—and what lay between long firm thighs—was to be devoted, well then, they were a *most* devoted couple!

"We were mad, were we not, Lavinia? The nights without sleep, lovemaking that melted into lovemaking, a flow of desire where even the resting was passionate. And how we suit, you and I. Mind and heart and soul. And how we fit, our bodies filling in and rounding out. . . ."

A draft of night air blew in from an open window. Laurence pulled the quilt over his shoulders.

They had come together as lovers and lovers they had remained, even now beyond the grave. For he would sleep and as it happened every night since Lavinia had died, he would take her and love her and his body would fulfill itself and she would call out his name with an exquisite cry.

He had told Anny: "Rest easy." Only in the invisible world between life and death, at night, did *he* rest easy.

Chapter Five _____

LAURENCE STOOD BEFORE the fire in the library. Mornings were chill even in June when it remained light the day round. It seemed no one except himself slept during this period. Whenever he rose, as early as four o'clock, the peat blocks were blazing, breakfast noises emanated from the kitchen, and it was never long before Anny appeared with the teatray.

"Vast halls are not for the likes of me," he said aloud to Murphy, who had positioned his black-and-white body as close to the grate as animal wisdom permitted. "I'm a nester, old friend. My books close at hand . . ." He moved slowly along the walls running fingers across the elegant leather bindings, gold-tooled. ". . . rooms of a dimension that warms quickly and cools equally fast." He knelt to stroke the dog's nose. Murphy sighed.

Pouring himself another cup of tea, Laurence sat down at his desk. He was far from eager for this first task of the day. Olaf was to have passed a message to Thomas Matheson that he was wanted at the Ness. The French ormolu clock had just chimed six. Whatever his sickness, the man was not a layabed, this Laurence knew.

He had not opened a book five minutes when Anny hustled in with the culprit.

Deal with him, Master Laurie. Her eye held the message. No doubt of the conversation between Anny and Olaf over late-evening tea.

"Thank you, Anny."

He closed the book and waited. Anny backed up to the hearth, where she took up an iron, poking at a fire that was clearly in no need of assistance.

"Anny, thank you."

Placing the tool back against the stone hearth she stood firm.

"Aye, Master Laurie." She lingered on the name.

Thomas had not moved from his spot to the side of the desk. His knotted hands played with the edges of his cap but his small eyes were steady. Laurence reflected how little the body changes in its essential configurations as it ages. As a child he recalled an obscure aversion to the man's lips. He had read cruelty in the corners pulled over the teeth. It was still there.

"Please shut the door behind you, Anny." The tactic was to match her stubbornness. The door slammed and Laurence knew it was a standoff—but chiding a man in front of another was not his way.

Visions of pitiably dismembered birds strewn across moor and path brought back the nausea, as when he had first encountered such scenes and heard his father passionately invoke God's justice toward one Thomas Matheson. "And he is far from stupid!" His father would shake a fist in the direction of the Matheson cottage. "He knows the difference between a stone and a living creature. He knows it *there''*—he brought the fist hard against his temple—"but it's lost *here.''* The hand fanned out over his heart.

Looking up at this same Thomas Matheson forty years later was proof enough: the old have years to perfect their inclinations. At the time he spoke with Olaf the visions had not yet crowded in before his eyes. Now he could not get rid of them. So. There would be little he could effect on this score. He certainly would not preach a lesson to this man. Some vital part of the mechanism that controlled Thomas's acts was missing. Of this he was absolutely sure.

"Thomas, I must demand that you not touch the ernes' nests again.''

There was no point in spelling out why. This would lead the discussion to questions of motive and consequences. Questions to which Thomas was perfectly capable of giving answers, and every answer would be a clever, consummate lie.

"I also request that you cease . . . cease . . .'' He hesitated. "That you try to cease strangling birds indiscriminately. Yes, Thomas''—Laurence responded to the furrowed brow—"yes, you understand the word.'' He allowed his voice full range as Thomas stuffed his cap into his pocket and pulled his left ear.

What is going on in the brain behind that ear, in that heart under the stained tunic?

The door flew open.

"Anny!'' Laurence stood up, ready to scold, but it was not Anny. It was Michael holding in his hand a tiny goldcrest. The bird's head hung down with a particular twist that meant only one thing: it had been strangled.

Ignoring Thomas, Michael shot across the room to his father.

"Father, where did this come from?" Fury and bewilderment mixed to bring a full blush across Michael's olive skin.

"Where did you find it, Michael?"

"On the chest outside the door."

"Which door?"

"*This* door, Father, just outside *this* door on the oak blanket chest."

"Thomas!" Laurence came from behind the desk. Only then did Michael notice the man on whose face was a grimace nothing short of gloating.

"Father! Why is Thomas here? Isn't this our time? Why is he looking like that? Father?"

Laurence stretched out a hand to calm him, but it was too late. Michael straightened his shoulders and marched up to Thomas.

"It is *you* who did this, Thomas? You've been killing birds! And I thought all the time it was the dogs and cats and I even screamed at Murphy. Lots of times!"

He thrust the bird under Thomas's chin.

"You shall be punished, Thomas Matheson, you *shall*. Anny and I will put a charm on you! Good magic punishes bad people and you are bad, you hear? *Horrid, horrid!*" The boy stared straight into Thomas's face. The man did not flinch. From lips tightened to a thread came a faint hissing.

Laurence felt the blood racing up his temples. Thomas was not steady in his feelings. He would not forget this scene—just the one he, Laurence, had been determined to prevent. He opened the door to find Anny and Olaf standing a ways back from the front stairwell.

"Come in, Olaf. . . . No, Anny; just Olaf, please."

"But Master Laurie!"

"A moment only, Anny." He shut the door as Olaf entered.

Oh, my love, my Lavinia, you would take my hand and kiss my eyes and soothe me. And soothe the others. You would make it right.

No! This was not time for reverie. Lavinia was not here. It was for him to deal with the unfortunate event.

Laurence sat down again at his desk.

"You have been warned a thousand times over the years concerning the strangling of birds. On this count I am resigned, there is nothing to be done. It is unfortunate that my son came on the poor creature while you were here. As to the eagle, I think it best you pay your full sentence by working for Olaf for three months. Not as fowler or cragman. He will decide where on the land you are needed."

Olaf nodded and motioned Thomas to leave with him. The gloating had never left the man's face. He shook out his cap, slapping it onto disheveled hair that hung down lank to his shoulders. Just as he reached the door he turned.

"On the chest, ye say?" The words were spit out to Michael.

"Ye be lyin'. I laid it far up the path. I be no fool, ye know that." This was addressed to Laurence. Then he was gone, Olaf with him.

In a moment Anny entered.

Michael leaned over the desk.

"I did find it on the chest, Father." Laying the bird down, he stroked its head with a finger. "Death is so still, Father, isn't it? Every part of the goldcrest is still here and nothing moved. Was Mother so still?"

"Michael, I beg you . . . Anny is here and I have a question to put to her. Leave us now."

Anny stood with her head back, chin thrust forward, defiant and defending, for she knew Laurence had scented her out.

"Anny, Thomas claims he did not leave the bird on the chest. Michael claims it was there he found it. We know Thomas lies, but if in this case he is not lying, the bird did not find its way there by magic."

"No, Master Laurie, I won't be sayin' that. But helpin' the magic along! He be needin' a true punishment, Thomas Matheson."

"You know Michael Magnus always comes to see me after his breakfast."

"Aye, I do. We all do."

Laurence smiled in spite of himself. They *were* a crafty lot.

"Am I correct in assuming you placed it there for Michael to find?"

"The laddie has a powerful say with you, Master Laurie."

"But Michael, as you know, becomes more than agitated at such things, killings for no reason. Strangling is a hideous death. And in his agitation he would lash out, would he not?"

"Aye, master, it came to my mind, the laddie's pain. But Thomas Matheson be needin' a lash out. Ye be too gentle. Always thinkin' what the Lady Lavinia would be thinkin' and doin'. I know." Her body swayed upward. Her mission, as far as she was concerned, had, in part at least, been accomplished.

"What you also know but did not act upon is that Thomas

Matheson is unsettled in his mind and heart. He is bright and quick, but ever since he was a child no one could predict what he would do, how he would act. His fits of anger, banging his head, strangling birds—you've seen it all, all these years. You understand what I am saying.''

"I understand, Master Laurie, but what seems past yur understandin' is that Thomas Matheson is full o' evil, evil as even the magic can't touch. So, I thought, this time I'd try a bit o' yur thinkin'. Put the bird where the laddie finds it. Then he comes to ye with the poor thing, all tears and such. Then ye see the evil o' Thomas, up close. And send him off the isle, off o' Unst. It's the only proper thin' for it; send him away, or one day he'll do a proper bit o' killin'. Mark me, he will!''

"Never," Laurence said, tucking the eiderdown close around Michael's shoulders and neck, "never chastise a man when others are there. It is a humiliation that does not bring about good; on the contrary. In this case, with an unfortunate like Thomas Matheson, who is a cripple spiritually, it only serves to strengthen his resolve against us.

"When you must chastise, as you will be called on to do after I am gone, or simply when you have something to say about which you feel strongly," he continued, "think carefully before you speak. And when you speak, do so as calmly, as simply, as possible. Save your passion for those you love, for beauty, for . . ."

"For thinking about Mother and how she loved us?"

It will never end. I must accept this. For me, never. And for my child, until he takes a wife, if he is lucky. And even then . . .

"What did you do with the goldcrest?" Laurence hastened to change the subject.

"I buried it. In the wood. Under the apple tree. Do you know why I chose the apple tree?"

Because Lavinia loved apple blossoms most among all flowers.

"Why?"

" 'As an apple tree among the trees of the wood, so is my beloved among the sons. Under its shadow I delighted to sit and its fruit was sweet to my taste.' Mother always recited that when we sat together under the apple tree."

"Love is as strong as death. Many waters cannot quench love, neither can the floods drown it. If I speak I shall weep."

Laurence could taste the words in his mouth. The ache was unbearable. He gave Michael another kiss on his hand, blew out the candle, and left.

Chapter Six _____

"AND YOU BELIEVE this position *en famille* will be the answer, what?"

Alexander's long, angular face took on a farcical look. They were sitting in the chapel, deserted at this morning hour except for the sacristan padding along an aisle with an unsteady bouquet of delphinium in a white porcelain vase. In the half-light the object appeared to Robert like an icon from Byzantium. The chapel itself was somber. Another of Alexander's eccentricities, meetings in the chapel. "Like to be seen in the right places," he once offered with disarming insouciance. "Actually I'm passionately fond of the carved woodwork; the stalls and rood screen are masterful, don't you think?"

They had been together for nearly an hour in the front pew, each with his tricornered hat on a knee. They had not met, here or elsewhere except for passing each other in the halls, since the soirée. It was Alexander who had sent a note of being "in extremis" concerning the well-being of his friend, and setting time and place.

"The answer to what? I told you, I'm tired of living in a few dark rooms teaching half-starved hopefuls who live in

even meaner conditions than myself. I've always wanted to
see Shetland. I've—''

''My oh my, how the ostrich does fly! Is it to be believed? You've been running about the city, hither dither,
meeting the ravishing Isobel unbeknownst to a soul! Quite a
feat, I would say!'' He pulled at his nose. ''Don't look so
astonished, O prudent scholar. I for one have been overjoyed observing your activities. And so, might I add, have
your other *true* friends, the ones who are not part of the
aspiring herd. Impecunious but prudent scholar, slightly
paunchy for his age, rather on the short side, thought to be
celibate, is seen in passionate embrace with the Lady Isobel
on the bridge of Balgownie and elsewhere. Not once, not
twice, but—''

The sacristan scurried past them, a finger to his lips.
Robert nodded then turned to face Alexander. His hat fell to
the floor with a soft thud.

''Impossible!'' His hands were awash with sweat, a reaction to strain he had suffered since he was a child. ''There
never was a soul around when we met, and those few in the
tearooms couldn't have known us.'' He rubbed his hands on
his thighs and reached down, returning his hat to his lap.
His mouth was as dry as his palms were wet.

''There is *always* someone around who *knows*.''

Alexander, no longer the jester, turned to his friend.

''Look here, if I, if we had told you what I have just
related, you might have stopped seeing her, the last thing
any of us desired. You had emerged, Robert John, made of
the same flesh and blood as the rest of us! What we had not
counted on was the inordinate power of your reason!''

''My reason?''

''Yes, my friend, your marvelous brain that can cut

through a Latin obscurity revealing its true meaning with one swift foray into the text. Using this same faculty, it seems, you have cut yourself off, with rapier swiftness, from your beloved and hence from any chance of living a passionately interesting life. What say you in your defense?''

''I say you judge without knowing all the facts!''

This was uttered in a furious whisper, bringing the sacristan back with his own fury at their lack of propriety.

Robert's legs were jelly as he followed Alexander out of the chapel. They walked into a noon light that for a moment blinded them both after the semidarkness.

''Don't I know the facts?'' Alexander closed his eyes. ''You forget, my parents and Lord and Lady Eglinton are *les bons amis!* And with my intimate knowledge of your nature . . . Though I must admit I had hope—not much, mind you, but still . . . I had hoped you'd stand your ground against the old tyrant. Ah, well.'' He dropped an arm around Robert's shoulders. ''Let me ask you something, from my own morbid curiosity: What *was* this reason that has caused you to adopt your present course of action? In *your* mind, of course.''

Robert had to sit down. Ahead was a stone wall set away from the walk. A mass of hollyhocks spiked up behind, shaded from deep-rose to pink to white. He sat in silence, tugging at his beard, for at least five minutes. Alexander next to him rested his elbows on his knees and twirled his hat.

''One,'' he said, resting on the word, ''would have to be a fool to take on Lord Eglinton. I was humiliated. The reasonable—no—the rational course *was* for me to withdraw. He does not want me for a son-in-law. He is powerful. I am powerless. He is wealthy beyond counting. I am poor. . . .''

"But highly considered and from a fine family," Alexander interjected, popping his hat onto Robert's head.

"Stop playing the idiot." Robert shook off both hats, leaving them on the grass. "I had no idea our meetings were common knowledge. All right, *all right*." He countered Alexander's stare of mock amazement. "Now that you have pointed it out I see how stupid I was to have assumed we might come and go unnoticed."

"Would you have cared? Obviously Isobel did not."

"I thought her parents knew of our meetings."

"No concern why she did not present you to her parents sooner?"

"I thought—" He blew out a long breath. "Frankly, it was intriguing, waiting for her notes designating time and place of each tryst. It brought excitement into my life. For God's sake, Alexander, you were the one, years ago, who first started calling me—with your habitual irony—'prudent scholar.' "

"Quite right. But mark you, it was not out of approval. I do not approve of your course in life. Well, so you see it as sound judgment on your part, giving up the fight, going off to some wild, ungodly jut of rock in the North Atlantic."

"What would you call it, then?"

"Do you want one of my cruel, hence honest, answers?"

Alexander reached down for the hats. Dusting them off, he set each one, with a ceremonious flourish, onto its owner's head.

"I'd say it was the coward's reading of a situation. Everything turns on interpretation. For another man, of more stalwart nature, the reasonable reaction would have been to sweep up the beauty in his arms, salute her father and mother with utmost civility, and be off! One is not humiliated, my friend, one *allows* oneself to be humiliated. Did she not come to you to plead her cause, offering to share your simple bed and board? Surely she did. . . .''

"I thought you scorned her, Alexander. That night you were dripping scorn when you advised me of her upbringing, her intelligence. Now you talk as if—"

"I talk to *you*, imprudent one. *I* am rational. When I see someone I respect making an ass of himself I speak up. There is one more thing, of a practical nature. Rent me your flat, will you?"

"My flat! What would you do with my miserable flat? You're living in splendor at home, aren't you?"

"That's just it. I've decided I need a *pied-à-terre,* as the French put it, away from the parental eye. You understand. Come, say yes. It will be of benefit to both parties. You can leave it as it is, leave behind anything you don't need. I can post on whatever you may forget or find necessary *up there*. And this way we're sure to stay in touch. Fifty pounds a year? By the way, how long do you intend to hide in your arctic retreat? The boy is ten, or nearly so? He'll be off to university in a few years, won't he?"

They passed through the entrance to Powis House, with its two Moorish towers. Just beyond was an obscure burying ground.

"Do you know, this plot marks the site of one of the ancient churches of Old Aberdeen? Saint Mary of the Snows. *You*," Alexander said, looming over Robert and shaking his leonine head, "will be no more than the site of a man if you don't give up that precious virginity of yours. What more can you ask than to lose it in marriage? Who but our prudent scholar could manage such a feat? What man can claim such an honor these days? Only women are expected to come to the bridal bed untouched. It's true King's College was originally dedicated to the Virgin, but must you take it *that* seriously?'' He paused, then grinned. *''Finis.* I've said it all, and you, as usual, have listened with noble politeness. It's decided, then. I shall rent the flat and we will stay in touch. In three days I'm off to Paris for the summer.'' His grin widened. ''Pleasure and research, you might say. I do wish you happy, Robert John.''

Isobel sat in her favorite boudoir chair, legs tucked under her. Her eyes were closed but she was far from sleep. Sleep had been illusive the past nights since she had walked out of Robert's flat. By the time she had arrived home she had eliminated one course of future action. She would not confront her father. It was true, he could have been more politic in expressing his views, but then he would have respected Robert far more had he sensed a challenge. He might even have come around—halfway only, but that would have been a sign of movement. No, she'd let it be, but one thing was sure. Never again would she enter a ballroom to watch young women sit dismally in groups by themselves, while their mothers took snuff and gossiped, while the young men ogled and compared. Never again would she put herself where there was clearly an embargo on good conversation. Perhaps this she would mention to her parents. *They* had educated her, they were proud of her mind, they saw to it that dinner conversation in *their* home sparkled, yet they expected her to rejoice in the company of those male bucketheads and female featherbrains!

Oh, there were some, a few, who were interested in

philosophy and theology, who read Ovid and Homer and the Bible for its poetic value as well as its religious exhortations, who came evenings to enjoy the music of Mr. Handel and Mr. Corelli, among others. But oh, they were *so* few. And then, like a gift from life, Robert had stood before her, brought there by the improbable Alexander the Great, and she understood, or thought she understood, that all had been a preparation for this love.

One thing fretted her, nagged her. She should have admitted it there and then, on the bridge. She *had* seen her father's choler when she had expressed more than ordinary interest in Robert's company after that fateful evening. She had suspected from the start that he would not consent. But she had counted on Robert's love being as strong as her own, to surmount even one as powerful as her father. She had not counted on his nature being that timid. How could she have known? No rendezvous was too daring, no time too early or too late, no request to audacious. He was always there.

Let him go to Unst. For the first time in her life she would wait and see. She would find an occupation to fill the hours, the days, the months—even the years, if it came to that. And she would see.

Chapter Seven ────────────────────────

ON A BRIGHT WINDY day the end of July Robert John
stepped aboard the *Erne,* docked in Lerwick harbor, after
forty-eight turbulent hours on a storm-tossed sea. His head
seemed to end somewhere in the air far from his body and
his legs still felt unsteady, though the water was now calm.
The young man extended an unsteady hand to Olaf then
quickly withdrew it, to wipe the palm against his doublet.

"My apologies." His smile was wan but ready. "I most
nearly gave you a sweaty greeting." Robert sat down and
lowered his head between his knees. "And a rather odd
one. I doubt I'll ever cross again! Two days on a roiling sea
is not for . . . Aiee." And he put his hands against his
throbbing temples.

Olaf shook his head in protest. "The laird has told me
much o' ye. He'd say ye be up to whatever be asked o' ye.
A press on the neck would be helpin'."

Robert looked up.

Olaf added, "It works mightily when the sea's too much,
even fur them that's spent their lives on it."

The young man let his head fall lower to the floor. He
drew in deep breaths of the sea air. There was nausea along
with the throbbing head. It was difficult to speak.

"It's kind of you, but . . ."

"But we've only just met. When would ye have me doin' it, when we're a year acquainted and ye be used to the sea?"

Olaf pulled off Robert's scarf and laid it on the corner of the bench. He massaged with firm slow strokes, against the bones behind the ears.

"If there's a need, Robert John, it's to be attended. We've no time fur hellos and howdeedos o' the city folk."

He shifted position, now in front of Robert, letting his hands spread over the skull, forcing the scalp back and forth.

Robert turned his head. Olaf's hands had indeed chased out the pressure. He was still nauseated but less so.

"I might try to get up now, if you please, Olaf."

Olaf guided him to an upright if shaky position.

"That's it."

"I'm better and I thank you."

Olaf rummaged through the bottom of a leather sack by Robert's feet. He was as tall as the laird, perhaps taller, broad through the chest and upper arms. Greying hair that must once have been the color of cornsilk flowed to his shoulders.

"I've fresh water here somewhere, damn it!" he said, pushing his face into the bag. "Could ye down a swig? I'll warrant ye've a squeezy stomach as company fur the head. Ah, here 'tis." He drew out a small pouch with a bone stopper.

Robert ran his tongue over his parched lips.

"More than company for the head! It's been my companion for two days. I've eaten nothing and drunk very little. I'll take the water with pleasure. And—" Another wave of nausea went through him, weak but very much there. "And might we put off this last leg of my voyage, for an hour or two? My head is better, but the belly!''

"The belly is twistin' like a pitlock on a hook. Aye, 'tis early enough and we be with the tide. We'll make the Ness by sundown, though in the night makes no difference. Would ye care to lie down, be with yur own thoughts, or have a walk about the port?''

"A walk, if I am able to manage it. And might I borrow your arm for a start?''

Olaf tucked his left hand into Robert's armpit and they started off the boat.

"There's no more to be done.''

Anny stepped back to survey the room.

"Whatever's been the tutor's lodgin's in Aberdeen, he'll have the sea air cross his bed at night and a mighty fine sight from his window, won't he now, laddie?''

Michael was fingering a small cut-glass inkwell set out on a silver tray in the center of a gleaming mahogany desk.

The boy looked up.

"I've never seen this before. Is it Father's?''

"Yur father's or his father's, I don't know. All these questions.''

Anny gave a tug and smoothed down the quilt that covered the bed to the floor.

"It's just waitin' to be filled with ink. Why be ye askin'?''

She came over to Michael and gave a tug to his vest, pulling it down around his waist. Then she pushed the hair away from his brow.

"Do ye fancy it?''

"It's like . . ." He paused and his hand closed around it. "It's like the top of the water sometimes. See." Michael held the ball up to the window, turning it slowly. "See, Anny, it's caught the light. It's beautiful. It's cold, too." He rubbed a finger on the facets. Then he placed it carefully back onto the tray.

"When will they get here?"

"When they *get* here and not a minute sooner, fur all yur askin' me a thousand times."

For days now Michael had been behind her, following every move; at times just sitting silently watching the preparations for Robert John's arrival. At other times the whys and whens and whats streamed from him, disconnected questions, but all coming from a corner of the heart where fears are hidden and nourished.

Laurence had left it all to Anny.

"Make the room attractive and comfortable. Whatever you need, we'll have Ivar make or fix it and Olaf can be recruited for shopping in Lerwick, if it comes to that."

He had then retired to his study and his solitary walks.

"Tryin' to forget the man till he's here, him, too," Anny had complained to Olaf one afternoon as he was unloading supplies.

"I'm tellin ye, Olaf, *I* can't be dealin' alone with the tutor. What if Master Laurie be pullin' in again, really pullin' in?"

Here Anny had planted herself directly in front of Olaf, as if he would find corroboration of her worry in her stance.

"Ye be dealin' with anyone!" Olaf had laughed and there the matter had rested.

But through the last weeks Anny had gone about with her own fears. More times than not, seeing a light beneath the library door long after midnight, she had stopped, her hand up to knock, only to shake her head and tiptoe off.

What was the use of it?

She knew her master clear through, as if his head were made of crystal like the inkwell. He'd taken the step, the one he'd been wrestling with for years. He'd put the child in another's hands. Anny knew it was more than difficult, for a man whose station in life had always allowed him complete control. But then he hadn't been able to save *her,* and this was the life blow.

Anny handed Michael a twig broom and moved the vase of flowers a little closer to the edge of the desk.

That be the life blow. Her thoughts were again with Laurence. She'd tell him, if it would help. She'd say, There's no one goin' to touch the fate o' this laddie. It's all written down. . . .

"Come along, my peerie lad," she said, smiling broadly, "we'll have a look outside."

Michael stood by the bed, holding his hands, palms down, about six inches over the coverlet.

"No." Anny spoke under her breath. "No matter who's to teach him, it's all been writ fur this child." Then, aloud:

"All right, all right, ye be sainin' the bed. Come along. Ye'll want to be right there when he steps off the boat, I'll warrant."

Anny knelt down in front of the boy.

"Or don't ye?" She scrutinized his face, pulling him to her. "Think o' all he's left behind. A whole life, I'm thinkin'. Friends, maybe a lassie he loves, his place o' birth. And ye? Why, ye be stayin' right here, right in the middle o' it all. Come now, it's ye must be givin' him a smile. He's the one be needin' it!"

At that moment Laurence came up the stairs to the mid-landing. The door was open. Michael was clinging to Anny.

"Here's yur father, laddie."

Anny stood up.

"Yur son's afraid the tutor might be spiritin' him away from us, Master Laurie." And she gave the man a look straight from his childhood, the same one he had seen her give his parents again and again when she was decided on her way.

He came up to Michael and laid a hand on his head.

"How could that be, Michael Magnus? I'm here. Anny is here. Olaf and Ivar are here." He bent over to kiss his son's forehead. "And Jaimie and Murphy and Swabbie, not to mention all the other creatures that have become permanent residents of the Ness! How could you ever be spirited away?"

He looked at Anny.

"You know Anny well enough. She would never allow that to happen. Never."

Anny answered with a flounce of her skirt.

"Think of it, between Anny and your tutor, you shall learn all there is to know in *this* world. Now," he said as the two walked through the doorway and slowly down the stairs, "are you not a fortunate young man?"

In answer Laurence felt Michael's warm fingers curl about his wrist.

Chapter Eight ─────────────────────

ANNY GAVE A STIR to her pot, a bubbling concoction of winter vegetables, chicken stock, and meat, left to simmer through the day.

"They've come, Anny." The boy's voice was at once breathless and wary. "Father went down to meet them. I said I'd get you."

"And so ye should, laddie," Anny answered.

She tucked a wisp of grey beneath her cap and untied a long thin piece of cloth wound around her waist.

"There." She patted her ample sides. "It's not much fur Anny to be ready!"

Then, considering the occasion, she pulled the draw-strings of her blouse and secured them into a small tight bow.

"And ye?" Anny walked around Michael. "Aye, ye be fine, just the way I put ye together this mornin'. Yur cheeks be a bit hot. . . ." She put the back of a rough hand over the boy's face. "Ye be mindin' what we talked. It'll be mighty strange fur him, comin' here, leavin' behind. That's what's hard, leavin' behind. Mind now, he's to feel at home." She took Michael's hand and with a sudden jerk pulled him through the doorway. "Soon as he's over the stoop, he's to feel at home. Nay, *before*. Soon as he puts a foot on the Ness. Mind now.''

With much protestation Robert allowed Olaf to carry off his baggage.

''And don't be worryin' about yur books.'' Olaf stepped off the boat ahead of the young man. ''I'll bring 'em 'round end o' the week.'' Olaf hoisted the strapped cases under his arms.

Laurence was standing by the pier, and behind him a boy and an old woman, hand in hand.

''This is Michael Magnus,'' the laird said. ''Michael, this is Robert John.''

The boy put out his hand and Robert saw a small flushed face turned anxiously up to his own. Like a flood the years came surging back over him and he was standing before his own tutor, frightened and fatigued.

''I'm pleased you've come, Master John.'' The boy stood straight and still.

''And I . . . young laird,'' Robert heard himself say. But the effect on all was more than he could have hoped had he planned the words.

Michael's face was radiant with the sudden delight of it. The woman clucked approvingly and moved in closer. Laurence turned, his eyes full of approval.

''And here is Anny Anderson, nurse to our . . . young laird.''

Anny curtsied.

''Welcome to Burrafirth, Master Robert John. We're hopin' ye be happy here and we'll do our best by ye.'' She curtsied again.

''Well done, Anny,'' Olaf called out. ''Ye see, Master

Robert, they'll be settin' ye in before ye be havin' a chance to change yur vest," he said, and he lengthened his strides toward the house.

"We'll not detain you from a change and a wash." Laurence started up the slope. "And a glass of claret. How was the crossing from Aberdeen?"

Robert fell in beside the laird and Michael took up his place behind next to Anny.

"The crossing was a rough one, sir. Even Olaf agreed— and for me, particularly so. I'd best find some other way of getting around your seafaring world."

"Did you vomit, Master John?" Michael came up beside him. "Because if you did, Anny has a tea *just* for vomiting."

"To make me vomit or to keep me from vomiting?" Robert smiled. "Or am I starting lessons too soon?" The young man looked to Laurence, who was thoroughly enjoying the exchange.

"It just show ye be feelin' at home," Anny said determinedly. "The laddie's right about the tea. It'll soothe yur belly. I'll have it ready by the time ye be washed and changed." She lifted her skirt and, with a quickness that belied her bulk, hurried off.

Olaf had already put down the cases in the hallway and was flexing his arms when Anny hustled by, calling over her shoulder for him to come into the kitchen.

"He's a lovely look, don't ye think? He'll do mightily, I can see it in his face. Poor lamb, and him without father or mother, the laird was tellin' me."

Anny filled the kettle from a bucket and hung it in place of the stewpot that had been simmering since early morning.

"Inside as out, he's a fine one," Olaf agreed. He opened the cupboard and took down five cups and saucers. "I'll take a cup with ye, Anny. I'll be stayin' with Ivar. There's some tack he's been waitin' for, comin' up from Edinburgh."

"He'll be glad o' that, what with four new ponies in the pen."

Anny poured some hot water into a large bone-china teapot, swished it about, then emptied it into a broad tin bowl.

"What did ye talk of, ye two? With the whole day together. If I know ye . . ."

"Aye, ye know me, Anny Anderson, since we be bairns, so rest easy. Ye've not to worry. He's a fine one. I saw it, I was watchin' him when I told him o' the laird's sorrow since the Lady Lavinia passed on. He's a heart, with all the learnin', so ye've not to worry."

Olaf peered down into a bowl where Anny had put tea leaves mixed with a powdery brown mixture.

"What've ye got there, one o' yur charms already ye'll be workin' on the man?"

"If I'd not sained ye when that abscess burrowed into yur neck, where would ye be now, Olaf Haroldson? No, ye know it, it's tormentil tea to settle his belly. It'll be good fur all of us, the way we been goin' 'round these last weeks."

She put down the spoon.

"Olaf, yur tellin' me true, I know. And I see him, but I've a pain what won't *go.*" Anny sat down by the table working her fingers against each other, her eyes closed.

"Anny Anderson, ye're not lettin' up *now,* not ye! Here"—Olaf pushed the teapot between her hands—"fill it up. They'll be waitin'. Nearly ten he is, the laddie's no babe. It's a start, Anny. Fur all o' us. A new face, a new heart, Anny. Will ye try? Will ye?''

Anny shook the dry herbs into the teapot and poured the steaming liquid slowly over the mixture.

"I'm thinkin' *right now,* Olaf, it be like the tea. It wants steepin', to be a good cup." She managed a smile. "I'll try."

Robert John handed his cup to Anny.

"It is a very special brew, Mistress Anny. I'm feeling much much better. Thank you."

It was comfortable, among these people. No doubt they were as wary of him as he was of them. Yet here, in this room, full of life, he would slowly come to know them, and already he was comfortable. Perhaps they, too, for they did seem at ease.

"Ye're ever welcome and I've always a stock in the jar, so don't by shy askin'." Anny started to reach out and touch Robert's arm, then let her hand swing down. Michael was sitting on a low stool beside the new arrival. From time to time over the rim of his cup he would dare a look at Robert.

"I'll take another cup, Anny." Laurence walked over to the cluttered table. He poured out more of the amber liquid, then picked up a large thin book. "Here is something that will interest you. John Brand's *Brief Description of Orkney, Zetland and Caithness.*" Laurence flipped through the pages with an index finger. "It will give you a good sense of the islands."

Robert took the books with thanks, got up, and straightened the muslin handkerchief around his neck.

"If I might excuse myself, I'd best freshen up before supper."

"I hope we haven't kept you overlong. This is Anny's welcome and we must indulge her." Laurence smiled as Anny threw back her head in mock irritation. "Michael will show you to your room. If you are missing anything, please don't hesitate to ask. Anny runs this establishment nearly single-handedly and not on the strictest lines, not since . . ."

"Not since Mother died." Michael came up and stood close to his father. "Father told me you have neither father nor mother."

The boy's eyes were suddenly dark.

Robert shook his head.

"So we must help each other, mustn't we, young laird?"

Michael watched Robert open his valise on the bed. He took out a white cotton shirt and shook it.

The boy walked to the window facing northeast, over-looking the firth.

"It's a watery smell, the air. I can't explain what it really is."

Michael leaned over the sill. Robert laid down the shirt and came over to the window.

Michael looked straight into Robert's face.

"Are you lonely here already, Master Robert? Because if you are, don't be. Anny says to think what you left behind, to come here. I would be very sad, but please, don't you be."

Then: "You can cry if you want to. Anny says every tear is a crystal come from under the water. That's where crying and laughing come together. Do you know what is under *my* firth?''

"What is under your firth?''

"Golden streets and palaces of shells and jewels floating like flowers, *everywhere*. My mother used to tell me stories about the people who live there. They live with the seals. They're very kind and play wondrous tunes and . . .'' Michael pulled his chin with a shy smile. "'Course, I've never seen them, only the seals. But they're there and they *know* what's happening up here. Did your mother tell you stories when you were in bed, just before you fell asleep?''

Robert sat down in a wide rocking chair by the hearth. Olaf had made a fire while the tea was being served. Now it was roaring, sending up long tongues of flame.

"My mother,'' Robert said, his throat suddenly constricting, "my mother often told me stories. She believed in a land of sunlight and joy in the green wood, as she described it.''

Michael curled onto a cushion by the chair.

"Please tell me your favorite story.''

"My favorite one?'' His eyes blurred as he heard a voice begin, in a light singsong tone with a lilt to it.

"Please.''

He looked down at his charge.

"'Connla and the Fairy Maiden' was my mother's favorite and now that I think about it, is mine also. At least, favorite enough, with a few others.''

The flames were greedily licking the last of the peat blocks.

"Connla of the Fiery Hair was son of Conn, of the Hundred Fights. One day as he stood by the side of his father on the heights of Usna he saw a maiden clad in strange attire coming towards him. 'Whence comest thou, maiden?' asked Connla. 'I come from the Plains of the Ever Living,' she said, 'where there is neither death nor sin. There we keep holiday always, nor need we help from any in our joy. And in all our pleasures we have no strife. And because our homes are in the round hills men call us the Hill Folk.'''

Robert felt a light hand on his knee.

"I like the story." The boy's hand brushed back and forth. "Do you suppose your mother is there?"

"In all these years," Robert said, taking the fingers between his own, "in all these years I've not dared think where she is, Michael Magnus."

"*I* think your mother is in the green, green hills and *my* mother is in a palace under my firth. What happened next?"

"That will be for bedtime. Come, let me finish my wash." He put a thumb on the boy's nose. "I think it wouldn't hurt for you to take a cloth to your face, which, I swear, attracts smudges to it, Michael Magnus, young laird of Burrafirth."

Chapter Nine _____

SEPTEMBER CAME ON and the hot scent of meadowsweet hung in the air. Michael gathered bouquet after bouquet of the creamy-white flowers till Anny was forced to call a halt with a stomp of her foot and as fierce a look as she could muster, which was not at all in her mood these days.

"I told ye, Olaf," she said as the two were taking a late-evening tea after the others had gone to bed. "I said it soon as I saw him, Robert John, with his look, and ye told to me, 'twas inside as out and we're both right."

Anny poured a generous portion of milk into her cup, a libation to her pleasure.

"Where'll ye be takin' 'em tomorrow, or do ye fetch Master Laurie?"

Olaf picked an apple from off the top of a bowl of rosy fruit.

"No, not till the end o' the week," he said, rubbing the globe along his sleeve. "These be beauties. There was still a load o' them over to Balta when I took the master yesterday."

Anny handed him a plate with a slim pearl-handled knife and repeated her question.

"I'll be takin' 'em 'round Hermaness, near Humla Stack.

Fur the seals. I've been keepin' this trip. . . . Ye know
why. Aye, it's a fine way this roamin' about the island. I
can see, it's givin' the Scot a feel fur his new home.''

"And givin' the laddie a slow workin' into the harness,
ye're also thinkin','' the woman grunted contentedly.
"Master Laurie knows, he's thought it all out.''

Anny reached for an apple slice. The pieces lay dripping
in juice, black seed in white flesh.

Olaf got up.

"I'll be checkin' the boat early morn,'' he said, and he
swept the last of the fruit into his mouth.

Anny took the muffler from the back of his chair and
twisted it around his neck, dabbing up the juice that was
running down from his mouth.

"Ye be worse'n the laddie fur eatin'.''

She gave the scarf a tug. Olaf pretended a loud choking
gulp.

"I know, ye be sayin' it's warm but the chill's begun. I
felt it when I went out before supper lookin' fur that foolish
Murphy of a dog. So go on and keep it about ye.''

"I've an idea ye think me foolish as that dog, Anny
Anderson. But I'll do yur biddin' same as I've done my
whole life, same as we all done.''

With Olaf gone Anny sat down and pulled the bowl of
apples in front of her. Taking a soft piece of homespun she
began shining the fruit, pushing the cloth into the little dent
on the top where a leaf or two clung tenaciously to the stem.

"Aye, it's all in the skin, waitin' it is. Waitin'.''

Around the bend they saw the seals. Olaf dropped an-
chor, not close but within easy view.

"This be yur first time, Master Robert,'' the skipper

commented, squatting beside him, speaking in a whisper. "A sight, eh?"

Michael sat in silence; his hands lay one on the other in his lap. The sun was high, a searing noon light.

Robert glanced at Michael. The smile on the boy's lips, if it was a smile, had a melancholy just behind it. His eyes, though concentrated on the seals, were clearly looking beyond.

For Robert John it *was* the first time. He had never been nor imagined himself part of such a world, or shared any creature's life—man or woman. Knifelike, the memory of Isobel and the pathetically few hours spent together cut across his heart. It had been dawning on him that although he had read many things, he had seen little, experienced little, and there was discomfort and excitement in the realization.

These were magnificent seals. Sleek, their dun coats so near the color of the rocks they might easily be missed. Some were carrying on a dance in the water, some in pairs, a few alone. Others would slip off the rock into the sea, diving and arcing as gracefully as an arrow, and then, a few minutes later, clamber back to their places with an ungainly lumber.

"*Phoca vitulina.*" Robert broke the silence. "Common or harbor seal. Smaller than its grey or Atlantic cousin, the brown spots—"

"*Stop!*" Michael's hands flew up to his ears. "Why did you speak?" Flushed to his scalp, Michael looked at Olaf, his eyes wild. "Why did he speak? He broke the spell."

Then to Robert he sputtered out a whisper:

"I wanted you to *see* them. You broke the spell. Please, I want to go back."

The last was spoken, despite the whisper, with an authority Robert had not seen in the boy before. Olaf looked at Robert and gave a slight movement of the head, a kind of signal to him, who by now felt his heart a stone in his breast.

"I would like to go home, Olaf."

Ignoring Robert, Michael walked toward the stern of the boat, pausing a moment by the lugsail.

"Please, Olaf, I should like to go home."

Robert lay deep beneath the eiderdown. He heard the door shut behind Olaf, who was making his night rounds. The window was wide open, the air crisp, numbing the end of his nose.

Winter cold by Aberdeen standards, he thought, pulling the coverlet higher and settling on his side, the pillows well under him to the shoulders.

Little more than a month ago he had come. How quickly life shifts! He shut his eyes, trying to imagine himself walking up King Street. The young man who had bought cakes from that same corner bakery for ten years, who had lived in that same middle flat for as many, who had not written a line to Isobel, where was he? As impossible now to return and find himself as it had been nigh on unimaginable at one time to go forward, to become another. That person was gone. He knew if he was suddenly required to leave this island, this house, this bed, it would not be the same Robert John who had come, fearful and exhilarated at the prospects before him. It would be one who might well have stood and fought. . . .

The incident by the seals earlier that day was back. Olaf must have related the event to Anny, for when she put down the broth at supper he felt a hand cover his—for only a second, but it had been there.

Michael had not spoken except to ask permission to take Murphy romping. After supper he had given a collective good night and gone directly to his room.

Robert stretched out a hand and raised the flame in the oil lamp by his bed. Then he sat up, the eiderdown tight under his chin.

Why *had* he spoken out? He could hear his words, that morning in Aberdeen when Laurence talked to him of reason and imagination. "I, too, am not *all* reason," he had cautioned his future employer. And yet when for the first time in his life he was confronted with a kind of magic he had found himself uneasy and had fallen back on the Latin name for seal and a comparison that even to his ears had sounded ludicrous at such a time, a total non sequitur in that world of water and stone and sky and sentient creatures. Before the ineffable he had spoken and right now he hated himself. Worse, had he not fallen back from another kind of magic? He had not written. He did not even know . . .

A lone gull cried out the watchman's "all well."

There was a stir at the door. Robert fastened the collar of his nightshirt and quickly opened a small book that he had placed under his pillow. He had no doubt it would be Michael's face peering through the crack.

"I saw the light."

The boy tiptoed up to the bed, candle in hand, its tiny flame flickering brightly in the cold air.

Robert couldn't help a smile. Michael hadn't been asleep either, and had probably been standing for some time in the hall.

"Have you something on your feet?"

Michael lifted a heavily socked foot then put the candle down on the bedstand.

"Are you staying up?" He asked the question with diffidence and anticipation.

Robert pointed to a stool by the window. When Michael had dragged it close to the bed and settled himself, he sat looking intensely at Robert, his face pulled in, his eyes at once heavy with sleep and attentive, waiting.

Neither spoke. Then:

"I think we are learning much about each other, you might say. Learning to live in each other's pockets, what?"

At the image Michael broke into laughter.

Robert put a finger to his lips.

"We'll have the house down on us."

"It was *magic,* you see, Master Robert, and you're *not* supposed to talk. That was why—"

"Why you burst out as you did. I'll accept that, young laird, but *you* in turn must realize how new, how strange it is for me. The seals, the stone stacks rising from the sea, shrouded figures. . . ." He hesitated. "Almost like prisoners waiting to break out."

Michael's eyes were bright now. The sleep was gone.

"They *are* like prisoners, aren't they? I never thought of that picture. I wonder who they are. Who do you think they are?"

"We'll talk about this another time. They are full of mystery, no doubt. But you must go to bed." Robert leaned on his elbow. "And I'll give you one line from Ovid to take with you."

Michael stood up and took the candle.

"'*In nova fert animus mutatas dicere formas corpora.*'"

'My mind is bent to tell of bodies changed into new forms.'

" '*In nova fert animus mutatas dicere formas corpora.*' "
Michael intoned the words as one would a benediction.

Robert held out his hand.

"Ovid knew many things. We'll give him more attention. Would you like this?"

Michael nodded, then started for the door, his "good night" barely audible.

He turned to Robert. "Some say the seals are angels out of grace with God. I think it's we who are out of grace."

And the young laird closed the door behind him.

Chapter Ten _____

LAURENCE RETURNED FROM Balta with more apples and a basket of pears. Just outside the house Anny handled the fruit as if each were a newly hatched chick.

"How is it, Master Laurie, our trees be spare this year?" The woman placed a small Bosque onto its bed of flax. The sides glowed pink, the overall green of the skin muted. "These be perfect, like the apples."

She set them down.

"Ye be hearin' from Olaf, how things go along here?"

"One question at a time, Anny."

Laurence flung off the oilskin he wore, rain or shine, when traveling by boat.

"That's better. Either this old cape grows heavier or I grow weaker. Now. Our fruit trees are resting through this season, I'm told, and Olaf did speak to me. But," he said, giving her a quizzing look, "there's usually enough left for you to tell. The week has passed quietly, has it?"

Delaying an answer, Anny leaned over to rub Murphy's belly. The dog was lying in his favorite spot by the stoop, all sun and warmth.

"Here's one who's always restin', like the fruit trees." Murphy lifted his tail a scant inch from the ground.

"Aye." Anny stood up and adjusted her apron strings. "Aye, it's been good. Master Robert started lessons the other day. We moved the oak table from the back room into the laddie's old nursery. Olaf's not about to begin studyin' now. . . ."

"And has it been quiet?"

Laurence stretched out his arm and Swaabie landed on his wrist, a thread of tang dangling from his beak.

"Quiet? Well now, that'll depend on what ye be callin' noisy, wouldn't it?"

"Anny!" Laurence gave his hand a twist and the gull flew screeching off. "Anny, come now. How has it been between them after the seals?"

Visibly relieved that he had been informed, Anny picked up the trove of pears and pushed on the door.

"I'll tell ye. But first off have a wash and I'll set up tea. The two o' them went rowin' to the other side o' the firth near an hour ago. The laddie knows a woodcock's nest hid away in one o' the caves, he says. If ye ask me, he's searchin' after those phalaropes again, but he won't say the name. Ye be washin' first off, Master Laurie."

Anny arranged her skirt and sat down on the sofa. Laurence was ensconced in his chair. The tea was amber, sweet and steaming.

"He was given a right surprise by the laddie's bein', with pardon, what ye be callin' uppity. But then, Olaf said they both had a lesson from it. He's not used to bein' around the magic, Robert John isn't, and the laddie's had it all his life. He's—"

"It's *not* for my son to read his tutor a lesson, Anny

Anderson. Good God, is this how it is? I'm gone less than a week—"

"Ye're losin' yur temper." Anny shook her head. "And ye have no need to go on like this. Nay, nor right, and I'm sayin' this fur all the years I've walked these floors. Yur son's a real stand to him, he's laird after ye, aye, in name already. Ye gave him that name. And Robert John, clever and good he be, has somethin' to learn."

"Learn *what,* good God?" Laurence stirred his tea vigorously.

Anny poured a bit of the hot brew from her cup into the saucer and raised it to her lips. Then she set the china plate down on a small inlaid table.

"Learn? That there's happenin's about the land, takin' charge, stirrin', doin', carin'. He's felt it, Robert John has. And so have ye, Master Laurie."

Anny got up and stood behind the chair, running her hand over the embroidery patches along its high curved back. She was struggling with a thought and when it came it was offered almost as a benediction.

"And so did *she,* Lord love. Ye're still fightin' with the magic, aye, blamin' it, Master Laurie." And the hand that had comforted for fifty years touched his shoulder.

Looking up into Anny's face, Laurence felt suddenly tired. Bone tired.

Anny read it in his eyes. "Ye're wrong, master. Ye're fightin' whatever took her, and it weren't the magic. Fight the evil, but not the magic. 'Tis not the same."

She moved in front of Laurence, her hand still on his shoulder.

"Ye've not been to the seals since she died?"

Laurence closed his eyes in answer.

"Well then, there'd be no harm in it, I'll warrant. And much good. She loved 'em, she did. Why don't ye go? Fur yurself much as fur her and the laddie. Why don't ye go?"

It was late when Laurence returned for a second time that day. He went directly to the library and pulled on the Turkish bell cord by the far wall. A few moments later there was a knock and Robert entered.

"Welcome home, sir. The others have long gone to bed."

Though Laurence seemed pleased to see Robert, there was, for the young man, an anxious melancholy in his look, strangely unsettling, echoing, Robert realized in the moment, a similar feeling in himself.

"Actually, before she retired, Anny mentioned that you might wish to see me."

"Anny is right."

Laurence smiled, but this only reinforced Robert's initial impression of a sadness, a fatigue coming from far within his spirit, not physical.

"I have been to Hermaness, to the seals," the laird said—all said matter-of-factly, yet yielding. "Michael Magnus has no doubt told you I've not been there, alone or with him, since my wife died."

Laurence poured himself and Robert a glass of decanted claret.

"It was Anny's push, you might say. To be again a part of what my wife passionately loved, of what draws my only son, and of what, I think, has touched you."

Robert felt his cheeks grow hot.

"Ours is an inscrutable world. Intriguing, with a landscape of shifting tone, mood. One is led, ever so subtly, to believe in what one cannot see or fathom, more strongly than in the actual world in which one moves and sleeps and eats.'' He hesitated. ''And loves.''

He motioned to Robert to sit, but he remained standing.

''I walked across the heather close by the cliff's edge. Sea, rock, air, bird, cloud, foam, wind, all were one. It does not astonish me that you, too, have felt it, though you are not island born.''

Laurence swirled the claret to the rim of the goblet. He gripped the crystal globe between both hands and, without looking up, continued:

''And while not astonishing me, I would implore you, try not to lose Michael Magnus to this world. Women may find comfort in the enigmatic, the contradictory, but . . .''

But men are required to dismiss what they cannot explain. They ignore it. Forsaking risk they forsake beauty and tension, quickening. Do not. From out of the past, his mother's words, long, long forgotten, exhorting him otherwise. Robert's hands became sweaty against the cool of the glass.

Laurence looked up at his companion.

''My wife, you see, would urge me to accept the mystification. She found great comfort in it. It pleased her that at any moment the magic, this vague entity, might impose itself on our lives. For me it turned out to be a brutal contingency and so it remains. One becomes too vulnerable. You see—'' His face was drained of color. ''I have already lost once. I simply cannot bear to lose again.''

The French pendulum clock struck the half hour.

''Come.'' The older man gave a short sigh. ''Fears spoken out loud are diffused somewhat, eh? You've said nothing.'' The smile was now nearly free of its former sadness. ''I know, I've not given you much chance. I wonder what you are thinking, for there is much in that head of yours.''

''I think you should tell Michael that you have been to the seals, sir.''

''I'll tell him in the morning. We'll take a walk.''

Laurence took the empty goblet from Robert and placed it on the silver tray next to his own.

''Strange. I have dreaded my son's eyes on me whenever the question of an excursion to Hermaness presented itself. Now I have been and returned and I dread his joy. He will expect some kind of miracle from my visit, and what miracle can there be?''

He walked to the window. The moon was full, the Milky Way a pebbled path.

''What miracle can there be?''

Chapter Eleven _____

My dear Alexander the Great,

This week marks one month since I arrived at Burrafirth. Too early to make any absolute prediction concerning my future, but not too soon to pass on to you (for whom instant judgments pose no threat!) my sense of the place and the people who are now my family, if you'll allow me the word that is anathema to you.

Perhaps it is more to your taste if I refer to them as a cast of characters, though I myself feel less an actor—or director—in a play than ever in my life. My employer calls Shetland and especially Burrafirth a land of shadow and light, one that evokes hidden worlds within the visible world. This is true. But I am finding myself overwhelmed by the sense—how shall I put it?—of this being, finally, the real world, if by real we mean composed of elements essentially untouched by man. Ah! I suddenly realize we might also use this as a definition of a magical world. Perhaps this is the power of Unst and Burrafirth. Being a prudent scholar I shall have to mull it over.

You know I have always abhorred displays of wealth, rather than states of mind, as a sign of class. Here one's state of mind seems to be what causes everyone to act from the poorest to the richest. My employer is the only rich man, however, whom I have met and I suspect this will remain so, as he is a recluse. Therefore I feel closer to the source of a person's action and I feel more secure. Even the animals go about with a firmness of purpose. Do I make myself clear? No matter. I'm finding, as I write to you, that it will serve a double purpose. It will inform both of us—eventually!

To begin with my charge, Michael Magnus. He is far more advanced in what we call formal education than his father realizes. Fluent in both the reading and speaking of English and Latin, it is clear he has been through the library on his own, as well as with his father. This, too, the laird seems not to realize, from staying much to himself since his wife died five years ago. Michael is at once a born skeptic and a man of faith, his own faith! I will give you an example. Two days ago we were sitting high on a bluff overlooking the firth. He frequents this spot often, alone. We often sit together in silence. Suddenly, his legs drawn up, his head between his knees—he is a handsome boy, tall for his age, thin, hair nearly black, thick and curly, almost Greek, eyes that are enormous by any standards—suddenly he turned toward me, chin still resting on his knees.

"Why, Robert John, are the same acts of influencing what we cannot see called religion when it suits people [not, mind you, suits the Church, which would have been obvious!] and called superstition when it does not?''

This asked with a confidence I have yet to ascribe to my own musings in this vein. At the same time it was a child asking, a boy of ten who sleeps with three fingers in his mouth and a square of silk under his cheek. (I've not asked but I'm sure it belonged to the Lady Lavinia, his mother.)

What did I answer, you ask? I answered that it was a most profound question, one requiring much thought. And that he should think about his own answer. After all, O great Alexander, I have not been teaching for six years without learning that to return a question with another is the most fruitful method for both pupil and teacher!

Now to the laird (I call Michael "young laird," which gives them all great pleasure!).

I can't recall if I described him physically to you, that day we met in the chapel. Bear with me, O great one, if I repeat myself. He is fifty, unusually tall for a Shetlander, though there is one other who stands as tall and that is Olaf, a fisherman by birth and trade who has for years now been the laird's rod and staff, advising him on estate business. Also his closest friend. The laird married when he was thirty-six and the Lady Lavinia sixteen. According to Anny the nurse (and true power, the final arbiter at the Ness!), they met when Laurence came to Edinburgh on business. It was, as you would put it, a *coup de foudre*. Her death has never been adequately explained. She was found lying among the seals, as if asleep. She never woke. Her death devastated him. He lapses into long silences, days long. Michael has grown used to this. He is a sensitive person. I do believe he knows that his father is suffering, thinking of the mother. Michael himself speaks of her often and with ease, though his eyes will fill with tears. The laird attended our college and was a brilliant student. I made a few— yes, prudent!—inquiries before I left. I am hoping I shall manage well with him. Strange, Alexander, that I should be concerned with what is going on in the hearts of people. Perhaps this is another of Shetland's powers. Perhaps Isobel . . . Never mind.

On to Anny. Anny Anderson, sixty-five, who came to the laird's parents when he was born and who is, as I said, the uncontested power in this little family. Anny blusters and fusses but her eyes and ears miss nothing. She is a good-hearted soul who can be as crafty as the next if the occasion calls for it. These people, Alexander, the crofters and fishermen, live close to the pulse of their land and sea and they had better, for were they not attentive to the vagaries of the seasons—nay, of every hour—they might well be without what to put in their children's bellies. So Anny rules the house and everyone in it, and anyone who comes near it! I've a sense there may have been a moment, years ago, when she and Olaf might have wed, but that is gone and they seem to live as a couple nonetheless.

Olaf! A peaceful Viking going about the estate with long steady strides, a leather tunic buttoned up to the neck, an immaculate handkerchief tied round his throat. Believe me, Alexander, we who pass examinations and stick our noses into dead tracts thinking we are rendering the past and present generation a service have no gain on intelligence. Book learning, perhaps. But native intelligence, why, this place abounds in it! Why, even the animals are sharp-witted! Do you know, there is a black-backed gull that warns the seals of the presence of hunters? Not only the seals, but the green cormorants are indebted to this ungainly bird, who usually attends them when they assemble on the rocks for drying. And to watch a sheepdog working the sheep is absolutely humbling! Yes, I know, you whose family has land and sheep, to you none of this seems other than ordinary; but to me, they are miraculous. You see, I was right when I told the laird I was not all reason. *I am not!*

Then there is Ivar, an ancient one who looks as if a breath would carry him away. He tends the horses and ponies and cares for the stables and mends the boats. And finally, all who live on the estate farming and caring for the stock and sheep and fishing. They say a Shetlander is a fisherman with a croft while an Orcadian is a crofter with a boat!

One more thing. This will appeal to your sense of drama. There is a man the age of Olaf and Anny, one Thomas Matheson, whom I have yet to meet, a fowler and cragman about whom the following story is whispered round the peat fires. First I must tell you that he has strangled and dismembered birds for the sport of it since he could walk. This will make credible the tale I am about to relate. It seems Thomas with a younger brother and father were climbing a treacherous bluff when it became apparent their rope would not hold the three of them. Thomas was ahead, so the story goes (all this having been witnessed by one solitary fisherman from a hidden cove). The father bellowed out some kind of order to his son that was to save them all. What Thomas did was cut the rope and down went father and brother to their deaths on the rocks below. Horrifying! Quite, but how to prove or disprove such an account? The fisherman claimed that Thomas removed the ropes and they have never been found. This summer he dropped a female eagle to her death, bound up with his own gaters! I should like to see him exiled from Unst, as would Anny and Olaf and the hundred or so others who call this part of the island home, but the laird will not hear of it. There is an element of pathos, says he, about Thomas Matheson. Pathos! The evidence speaks to Thomas causing pathos, terrible pathos, one of these days. I intend to keep a sharp watch.

Write to me. You are no doubt at this moment lying in the arms of one of Paris's beauties. Take care she does not ensnare or infect you!

Pace, Robert.

Mid-August
Aberdeen

O Voyager upon Far-Flung Seas!

I pray you are not adrift but have come upon hospitable shores and are now tucked into the bosom of the laird! Forgive me. I am returned, having aborted my visit in order to prolong my life! Except for this one brush with an old Count (Fart) whose wife I must tell you is the tastiest morsel I've yet to sample, I went about as Milord Anglais! (As the saying goes, the King creates a nobleman but it takes four generations to produce a gentleman!) Yes, well, his Milord Anglais opened all doors and—quite right, old fellow!— all beds for me!

Quelle ville! What a city! Theatre, music, dancing, why there is not an hour of the night or day one cannot find entertainment in full! As to the women, O prudent scholar! Though I have been often enough to this city of love and lust, never . . . Truly, I am exhausted! Married women are the most demanding. They leave the marriage bed in a feverish state of desire. . . . I am convinced the husband is the true friend and accomplice of the lover! These women arrive with such heightened passion it is a wonder to behold, as well as enjoy! You see I have not had to frequent a brothel, either of quality or the more common (and more interesting) variety. Which of course decreases the chance of infection. Think of it. Not to have to interrupt the climax, but to thrust forward at the very moment of release, deeper into the glistening cave, pursuing the animal until its cries give way to pantings that leave the hunter and the hunted limp, sweated out! Yes! There is nothing these married women will not try; one need not dream of the wiles of the prostitutes. And they have a way of protecting themselves. What is wrong with our gentlewomen, that they treat a man's tool like the handle of a teacup? I smile, dear friend, as I ask *you* the question. Do you know the location of your tool, let alone for what it is used?

> Je ne prise point tels baisers
> Qui sont donnés par contenance,
> Ou par manière d'acointance:
> Trop de gens en sont parçonniers.
>
> On en peut avoir par milliers,
> A bon marchié grand abondance.
> Je ne prise point tels baisers
> Qui sont donnés par contenance.
>
> Mais savez vous lequels sont chiers?
> Les privés, venans par plaisance;
> Tous autres ne sont, sans doutance,
> Que pour festier étrangers.
> Je ne prise point tels baisers.

I shall translate it, for my own amusement, not for your edification!

"I think nothing of such kisses as are given by convention, as a matter of politeness; far too many people share them.

"You can have them by the thousands, cheap enough and in abundance. I think nothing of such kisses as are given by convention.

"Do you know the ones I value? Secret ones, bestowed in pleasure; all the rest are doubtless nothing but a way of greeting strangers. I think nothing of such kisses!"

I am writing this at your desk, having settled in last

night. You do live a Spartan life! I shall cover the floors with Turkish carpets (my parents have them piled high gathering dust in the attic!), tear up your sheets for dusters, and provide a new two or three sets. My God, I shall bring a dowry to this sorry little flat and make it smile! Of course, none of what I have written so far is of genuine interest to you! What you are waiting for is news of the ravishing Isobel. Am I right? Of course I am right!

I have not seen her! Her parents dined with mine two nights ago; I had not yet landed. What my mother told me was that she, Isobel, is contemplating a change, to Edinburgh, that is, if one may call that a change; though yes, we must admit it, Robert, Edinburgh does make us look like country mice! There lives in Edinburgh a sister of Lord Eglinton, who though she is his image *en femelle* has none of his morbid characteristics and many of his good. Yes! We must be charitable and admit the man is a genius in business affairs, of the first order of intelligence, handsome in a flaccid sort of way. You cry *Halt! Stop!* I shall. By my nonchalance I shall procure the address and send it on to you. If I were to ask outright, my mother would either warn Lady Eglinton that I am on the prowl or take the question as an oblique proposal of marriage to the fair one! Speaking of posting on, here is the fifty pounds for my nest. I look forward to neighborly encounters. You cannot imagine how refreshing it will be to open the door myself into my own abode! By the way, I am having the chimney swept tomorrow, the mantel repaired, and a new grate installed. Not a word! Someone has to care for you!

Salute to Ultima Thule. *Et à bientôt, jeune homme.*
Écrivez-moi, S.V.P.
Alexander

Mid-September
Edinburgh

O Crofter!

As ye sow, so shall ye reap! Yes, well, I have your
letter before me. As you see I am in Edinburgh since
two days. *Not* in hot pursuit of your beloved, though
why not I cannot fathom! You have a strange way of
taking hold of a fellow's loyalty, O prudent one, even
a fellow with as little taste for phantoms such as truth,
goodness, loyalty, the Soul, etc., etc., etc., as I. I will
comment *tantôt* on your epistle but first I will give you
news of the fair Isobel and her address where you
may, I pray, send on your genuine regrets for having
been such a pigheaded ass. There's an image!

I am staying with a cousin, Nicky Galloway, in
Forseter's Wynd. And who, may you inquire, resides
two doors away? None other than the sister of Lord
Eglinton. Margaret, it seems, reigns supreme and is
judged either formidable or majestic depending on
whether you are in or out of favour with the lady.
There now. You have Isobel's address. The house is
number 3. It is six stories high with wooden-faced
gables effecting a piazza below. I've no doubt I shall
very shortly come on Isobel in the street or at a soirée
(detested, to be sure!).

What I have heard is that she has taken up working

with the blind at a school for the same. Established, it seems, by a gentleman whose daughter married a Shetlander. Correct! The father of your laird's young wife. And she, our Isobel, is setting this Edinburgh society on its head by forming a circle of women similar to the Society for Encouraging Art, Science, and Industry, which is exclusively *male!*

She claims all three are the purview of women as well as men. Their first speaker will be a Mr. Thomas Sheridan, who will lecture on Rhetoric and the Art of Speaking! Do you think I should attend? It is open to the public. Plucky girl! Truly you are an *ass!* That's my news.

I shall stay here till the beginning of term then back to our snug flat and our pimple-faced ignorami! Each year just about this time I am tempted to hand in my resignation and become the gentleman farmer my father dreamed of. The hazards of being an only son! He must inherit, go into the army or navy, be a minister, succeed and fail all at once in order to satisfy his parents' aspirations and despairs. Parents are nourished by both, you know.

Now to your little family. I am seduced by them! Whether they are all as intriguing as you describe is another matter, but who could contemplate such a variety in the frozen north? Up to now I imagined Shetland populated by seals and polar bears and an occasional papist who had lost his way! You see, I have done a bit of research of my own. It has a most romantic history as well. Did you know these islands were once the property of the Kings of Denmark and Norway, and came into Scottish hands through a father defaulting on the dowry for his daughter? (So beware!) Around 1460 Christian, King of both Denmark and Norway, married his daughter Margaret to James the Third of Scotland. Finding himself without the florins to pay "up," he first ceded Orkney then Shetland to the Scottish throne, *et vous voilà!* So far north and still on Scottish soil! Think of it! You are as far from me as from the coast of Norway. Does this not give you pause? Perhaps you should push on, wrap yourself in a skin, and get yourself into one of those kayaks in which it is said the Finns (a magical people) float about in those northern waters. Where they come from, where they go to eat and sleep and fornicate, no one knows! They cause all sorts of wondrous things to happen. Don't ask me what they are! But enough, Alexander! It is you, Robert John, who should be telling me these tales. You are up there, in touch with the true source of all things, you tell me. I am impressed!

Now I shall hold fast to my reputation for snap judgments. Laurence the Laird. A prime example of what happens when one marries for love, though that is exactly what I am advising you to do! Yes, my boy, one dies before ever one has lived if one does not risk. Loving is risking, is it not? I have not yet found the one worth my risk, but when I do, you shall see the heavens lit up as far as Shetland and it will not be by the aurora borealis! Michael Magnus. Obviously enchanted at birth. Listen to his pronouncements. Mind him well, O prudent scholar. Anny and Olaf. A mix, thank God. Thomas Matheson. I'm rather drawn to Thomas. If the story is true, it takes stomach to walk back into the village *sans frère, sans père, sans* rope, *sans* everything! And haven't we all itched to dismember someone we know, haven't our fingers ached to tear and throttle? We are a bit of all the elements and all the fluids of this earth and so we love and hate and hate and love. Enough again. I have no intention of preaching you a Sunday Sermon. Just do something before she is swept off by one of the elegant wealthy interesting fellows in which this city, unlike Aberdeen, abounds!

Pace to you, *votre ami*.

Mid-October
Burrafirth

My friend Alexander,

How well you understand me! It does comfort me to know of Isobel's whereabouts, though God knows what I shall do. . . .

I am very much taken up with educating Michael Magnus. When I think what a sponge is this boy of ten and what mental layabeds the vast number of our students . . . When we are not at formal studies—Greek, Latin, French, mathematics, natural philosophy—we are everywhere, learning from nature. Then Michael becomes the teacher and I the pupil.

My education has not been without pain. As a matter of fact, a month ago something happened concerning the seals and Michael and magic that jarred me out of a complacency of which I was unaware. As you know I have always fancied myself the perfect blend of scholar-humanist. Meaning what? Meaning, I suppose, that I know when to listen to my reason and when to answer to my heart. You laugh! Because, you shout, I surely have been deaf to both on the subject of Isobel, and I have listened only to my pride. You are right, but as you see, pride has me in its vise. So be it—for the moment.

We are schooled, Alexander, *not* to risk. We are taught never to be in a passion, never to allow ourselves to be taken over, by whatever! Here, in Unst, I say again, I am taken over, by the eminence of the cliffs, the grandeur of the horizon, the colours of the sea, the secret ways of animals and birds. The wonder is, I am not afraid. I do not feel out of control. Is this a beginning? Tell me that it is, for one as prudent as I.

Your Parisian foray sounded quite grand, especially that you emerged unscathed. What else? Just thank you and should you see Isobel, tell her—no, tell her nothing. I'm not at all surprised at her activities. I think perhaps I was a ''cause'' for her, as she was obviously quite bored with her life in Aberdeen.

> *Toujours Pace,*
> Robert

Chapter Twelve

ON A GLOWING OCTOBER noon Michael and Robert climbed from the Ness to the cliffs above, where below the firth lay in a golden stillness. Across, the rocky landmass rose higher and spread wider than their own, but the two extended an almost equal distance toward the north and the open sea.

The few bonxies that had not already left soared and swooped, waiting for other birds to drop their prey. The sky was steel-blue and the clouds were handfuls of wool sheared from sheep.

The boy held fast to Robert's hand.

"And beyond my firth, what is there, Master Robert?"

"Beyond? Why, the grey icy waters, I would guess. And the Artic, where the polar bear swims beside ice floes bigger than Shetland. Bigger than Scotland." Robert smiled down at Michael. "But right here is all the beauty we need, especially today. Come, we've time to sit."

With legs outstretched and arms supporting their bodies, the two sat and watched.

"Tell me a tale, please." Michael rolled over and pushed his nose into the mossy turf. "Tell me the fairy maiden story, the first one you started that first evening when you came. You never finished it.''

"That's right, I never did. With all the others, and all the talking you do in bed!''

He lay back, and in what Michael called the ''telling'' voice, began.

"When the maiden ceased to speak, Connla of the Fiery Hair rushed away from them and sprang into the curragh, the gleaming straight-gliding canoe. And then they all, king and court, saw it glide away over the bright sea toward the setting sun. Away and away, till eye could see it no longer. And Connla and the fairy maiden went their way on the sea and were seen no more, nor did anyone know where they came.''

Michael was lying on his back with his face to the sun. The moment Robert finished he was up, cheeks blood-red.

"Would *you* go with her, Master Robert? Would you?''

The tutor looked at the boy's intense expression and realized that in his own chest, his heart was racing.

"Would you go to the green hills? Because that's where they went. Maybe''—he hesitated, biting his lip—''maybe they went to the kingdom under the sea, but anyhow, would you go with her?'' .

Two months ago, it was suddenly clear to Robert, he would have answered a resounding ''no!'' Now . . . His chest was bursting.

"Aye, young laird,'' he said, ''aye, I would go with her.''

"But I would not!'' Michael shook his head fiercely. "He shouldn't have left his father and no hearing from him again!''

"It is a tale of fairies, Michael Magnus, you know this.

Connla chooses, gives up everything for the maiden. How would you have it?'' he asked the boy, and there was intense interest in the question, for Robert had learned early on that the boy's wonderings were not to be scoffed at as childish or sentimental.

''Well-l-l''—Michael drew out the word—''if it *is* magic, and it *is*,''—he swept the air lightly with his arm— ''I would have her bring the magic *here*, to share. Then Father wouldn't be alone. Mother would do that. Mother. . . .'' His voice was barely audible. ''She would have kept the magic here. She has, actually, though she's gone. I would keep the magic here, for her and Father.''

Robert looked at the firth. The water was a covering of tinted glass. Putting his arm around the boy's shoulder, he said, ''I wonder if you have not done so already. I wonder if you have not!''

More than five years passed. Michael Magnus had grown tall and as comely as Connla, Robert commented one morning when the boy skidded in and out of the kitchen, grabbing a piece of fruit and shouting back his thanks.

''And he be com . . . comel . . .''

''Comely, Anny.'' Robert smiled. '' 'Pleasant to the eye,' is what it means.''

''Well, he is comely in heart, if that's it.'' Anny opened an iron door midway up the hearth wall, revealing four loaves ready for cooling. The room smelled of peat ash and crusty fresh-baked bread and chicken laced with herbs stewing on the hob and apple blossoms trailing from a shallow dish in the center of the table. The sixth spring of Robert John's life on Unst was in full array.

Anny tucked her hand into a mess of cloth, winding it glovelike around her fingers.

"He's like his mother, Lord keep her."

She set each loaf onto a board along the window seat directly across the oven. Robert, perched in a corner of the pillowed ledge, put his nose against the hot crust with a approving sniff.

"And like his father. The laird is a handsome man, Anny. And generous. And kind. He's been more than understanding with me these last years."

"Aye, he looks to ye as a son. No, it's not so much generous, I'm thinkin'. Generous comes from both o' them. No, it's the laddie's *way* with the livin'. Birds and beasties and what's quickenin' up from the earth. Us, too; he's got a way with us, too." She stopped by the table. "Though he's a stubborn one at times, he's got a way, Master Robin. He's like her."

"Well, whichever parent he takes after, he is quite intelligent. Out of the ordinary! There are nights I don't catch a wink, preparing texts and examinations for him." Robert took a small knife from his pocket. He pulled the sheath and the scraping drew Anny instantly to her loaves.

"Don't ye go touchin' that bread, Robin lad! I been wonderin' where the laddie comes by his ideas." Her pretended rage ended in a tweak of Robert's ear. "Ye've a mess o' springy heather on that head o' yurs, ye have." Anny stood away admiringly. "Aye, but ye're lots tougher'n when ye come and yur color's no end brighter."

She paused, scratching the corner of her forehead.

"Aye, he's his mother, head to toe."

A sudden yelp brought Robert to his feet and both to the window. If Michael resembled his mother, there was no denying her beauty. Robert could see Murphy at the end of a stick, both intent on a tug-of-war. Michael's hair fell across his forehead and to the sides full over his ears in soft waves. He was already far taller than Robert, nearer his father's six feet and more. The cheekbones were high and fleshed, the chin squared off with a distinct cleft, the nose thin and long, flaring slightly at the nostrils. But the feature against which no one had protection was his smile. Even Murphy seemed to give way under its radiance. Eyeing his opponent through half-closed eyes, he dropped the prize and the two were rolling over an emerald turf unspoiled by scrub. Murphy's yips of canine ecstasy and Michael's laughter sent a chattering of starlings over the rooftop.

Robert slipped the knife back into its sheath. He started for the door then stopped as he felt Anny staring him down.

"It's a powerful ache, Master Robin. In *here*."

When he turned, Anny was clutching the panel of her smock.

"First off yur comin' set me fearin' I'd lose him. Then ye turned out no more'n a boy yurself, with no mother and a heart big as Unst. But now, with Master Laurie sendin' him off, he'll be truly gone, from all of us, Robin."

And she was down on her workstool, head in hands.

Laurence had cautioned Robert only the evening before that Anny viewed Michael's going to Oxford as exile, for him and for herself. She had counted on Robert's tutoring to keep Michael at home.

Robert took Anny's hands away from her cheeks.

"Firstly, did not your master go to King's College . . . and return?"

Anny pulled her mouth into a thin line.

"Well, didn't he?" Robert persisted. "Yes, he did, and

he returned. Secondly, *he must go*. There is much for him to learn that I cannot teach him. And most important of all, he needs to meet people, young men and women of his own age. Do you realize, Anny, we are all he has ever known, we who inhabit this house and the estate, vast as it is? True! And an occasional traveler from abroad. He needs new faces and ideas from fresh, worldly minds. He'll return. How could he leave Burrafirth, Anny? I promise, we'll manage and he shall return. I gave Michael *our* word, that we will care for his father, the animals, the birds, and—and the seals." The last was spoken softly. "We'll manage and Michael shall return."

Outside, the frolicking ended as Murphy left off licking Michael's face, trotted over to the stick, and headed for the other side of the house to gnaw away undisturbed. Michael lay on his back, hands folded across his chest.

How he would miss them, all of them! And the firth. He had only to shut his eyes, no, not even that, to navigate every inch of it—caves, grottoes, dark coverts by the water's edge, stacks, all. And the seals!

He hadn't been sleeping well and last night's slumber had been continually broken by dreams of his mother. One memory kept insinuating itself.

"When you are laird in more than name," she had said, holding him close against her breast, "there will be another inheritance coming to you. In its own time. When it comes you must keep it in absolute trust." Her hair had fallen over his face, leaving the scent of lavender that in this moment he could taste as well as smell.

"The seals must never be disturbed."

Michael ran a hand across his eyes. His mother had leaned even closer over him, rocking him back and forth.

"And I will tell you why, my love, my own."

"Because!" Michael swung onto his knees, repeating his mother's exhortation. "Because the seals guard the magic, my love, my own."

He could feel the cool white of her neck and see the cresting upper curve of her breast as she pressed him close.

Anny and Master Robert and Olaf would keep the vigil, he could depend on this. And when he returned it would be time.

Anny lifted her head and dried her eyes on her smock.

"No, he wouldn't be leavin' his firth, would he now?"

Robert was grateful that the thought comforted her.

"It's part o' him, same as it was fur her. Why, the laddie spent more time on that water than he's spent on land. Least until ye came, Robin. Aye."

Anny went over to check her bread with renewed vigor. "Now I'm thinkin' on it, he said to me th' other mornin' when we went down to the stables, he said, 'Ye and Master Robert take care o' the seals fur me. I told 'em I was goin' away fur a bit, but ye must be sure no one hunts them. Father goes about so little these days, and Thomas Matheson is still doin' those horrible things.' And then he put himself in front o' me, solemn-like, like I never seen. 'I told them Father *might* visit them again,' he said, 'but we know he won't, Anny.' Then . . ."

Anny put a hand to her face.

"Then he kissed me!"

"You're blushing, Anny! It's not the first time Michael has kissed you, is it?"

"Aye, I'm blushin', Robin lad, fur when I looked at him, it was a grown man I seen, sudden-like, towerin' over me, all bright he was with the sun on his hair and his eyes clear like the firth. *Her* eyes, Robin, and talkin' about the seals. Oh, it's hard.''

Robert tucked a hand through Anny's arm.

''I'll wager Michael will master in two years what others take the full four years to learn. And there's plenty of work for us here. The laird is tired and now stays so much by himself. We'll all be looking after things more and more. And the house needs repairs, all the linen should be replaced. There won't be enough hours in the day to miss him.''

Anny patted Robert's hand.

''Ye be good fur me, ye be. But I'll tell ye, we'll miss him more'n ye think. Ye'll see.''

Robert walked slowly back to the library where Laurence had been working through the week on accounts with the inspector for the crown.

Cowardice or love, which was it? As much as he knew Laurence wished him to stay, needed him, Michael's leaving was a legitimate reason for him to voyage back. To Isobel? If she was not yet wife and mother. He had not written to her. And because of this he had not continued a correspondence with Alexander, who, after a few caustic notes, had also fallen silent except for the fifty pounds a year. These Robert acknowledged, but no more. Nearly five years and no contact. Aberdeen, King's College, Alexander, Isobel, and Edinburgh were now as alien to him as he surely was to them! Five years! Precisely like a pitlock through the hand. Perhaps he should now write to Alexander. Have the courage to break the silence. . . .

Love or cowardice? Both. Nothing was simple, let alone one's sentiments! This he had learned, living among those whose sentiments needed no divining rod to be tapped. He loved them and he loved Unst.

And he was afraid of what he would find, should he return.

It wasn't time. Even though close to five years had passed. If he still was hesitant to reach out to her, *it was not time*.

Chapter Thirteen ───────────────

Mid-June
Burrafirth

Alexander!

Yes, you are furious! And you consider not answering this letter! *You* have cause. But somehow *I* have hope!

The best is to begin with the here and now. Would you not agree?

Michael will be fifteen in October and has matriculated at St. John's College in Oxford. *Horreur!* you cry! That may be but it is now done. The choice came about when we had a visitor from London whose three sons were all studying there. This man, with force and charm I must admit, held Michael spellbound recounting the following story. It seems St. John's founder, Sir Thomas White, a London merchant, had been guided there by a dream, a dream of elms and ruins. Finding the remains of an older college, St. Bernard's, which had been established in 1436 by Archbishop Chichele for Cistercian monks, Sir Thomas built anew. Because of the dream Michael has chosen to study there.

The entrance examination? They have waived it, writing that it is rare to welcome a young man from this quarter of the country. What they have found rarer still is the quality of the essays in Latin, French, Greek, and Hebrew (Bravo!) that Michael submitted. So it is decided. His father will accompany him to Oxford the end of August. Don't be *too* horrified. It is one of the best of the lot, St. John's is. Old Archbishop Laud, who was president from 1611 to 1621, was a great benefactor and raised the standards mightily. We shall see.

You were also correct in your estimation of the boy. He was ready to enter University at thirteen but both his father and I deemed it wiser to keep him at home a bit longer. He is a blend of child and man still (and will, I think, always be so), but the child often overshadows the man. His bursts of passion are less frequent, but still close under the skin, ready to blaze when he is aroused. He is aware of this tendency and tries hard to brake. But he has temperament; you would like him, Alexander. You two would suit. He could take you on, unlike myself! Oh, as I write to you I realize how very much I have missed your letters, and your person! You do have a penchant for letter-writing, you know. And though you scorn it, you have a gift for living. I am slowly acquiring one.

You probably have seen Isobel numerous times over the last years, so you know I never did write to her. Perhaps you are both married by now, even parents! Please put aside your fury and write. I long to hear.

> *Pace,*
> Robert.

P.S. Enclosed, a four-year course of study suggested by an anonymous Oxford don. Philosophy every morning and evening. Classics in the afternoon. Divinity on Sundays and Church Festivals. Recommended Books:

First Year

Philosopical	Classical
Wingate's *Arithmetic*	Terence
Euclid	*Xenophontis Cyri*
Wallis's *Logic*	*Institutio*
Salmon's *Geography*	Tully's *Epistles*
Keil's *Trigonometria*	Phaedrus' *Fables*
	Lucan's *Select*
	Dialogues
	Theophrastus
	Justin
	Nepos
	Dionysius'
	Geography

Second Year

Harris's *Astronomical*	Cambray *On*
Dialogues	*Eloquence*
Keil's *Astronomy*	Vossius' *Rhetoric*
Locke's *Human*	Tully's *Orations*
Understanding	Isocrates
Simpson's *Conic Sections*	Demosthenes
Milnes' *Sectiones Conicae*	Caesar
Keil's *Introduction*	Sallust
Cheyne's *Philosophical*	Hesiod
Principles	Theocritus
Barholin's *Physics*	Ovid's *Fasti*
Rohaulti's *Physics*	Virgil's *Eclogues*

Third Year

Burnet's *Theory*	Homer's *Iliad*
Whiston's *Theory*	Virgil's *Georgics*
Well's *Chronology*	Virgil's *Aeneid*
Beveridge's *Chronology*	Sophocles
Ethices Compendium	Horace
Puffendorf's *Law of Nature*	Euripedes
Grotius's *De Jure Belli*	Juvenal
	Persius

Fourth Year

Hucheson's *Metaphysics*	Thucydides
Newton's *Optics*	Livy
Gregory's *Astronomy*	Diogenes
	Laertius
	Cicero's
	Philosophical
	Works

Mid-July
Aberdeen

O So Slow to Mature Scholar!

Of course I am furious. Nor would I be, had you not by some hidden byroad found your way into the high-walled manse I call my Life. Remember we are never as angry with those for whom we care not a whit as with those we love, which is of course the reason the fair Isobel shouted you down when last you saw her. Yes, we have spent a good deal of time together. Be glad I am prudent for once! We enjoy each other's company. I amuse her. She claims that my conversation is stimulating. Excellent, it occurred to me early on. I shall keep an eye on her, win her confidence so that she does not end by making a fool of herself with

some shrewd dandy! For they all are dandies no matter
what their mental capacities!

How and when do we meet, the fair Isobel and
Alexander the Great? She spends the "season" in
Edinburgh, which means from November to February,
and then she is back in Aberdeen. I manage to be
invited to my cousin's for Noël and *le Jour de l'An*,
which I extend into weeks!

I must say, old fellow, that remark you made so
long ago about being a "mission" for Isobel was un-
fair in the extreme. Knowing you to be *au fond*, a
kind, generous type, I can only surmise that you were
actually describing how you see *yourself*, which is not
generous! Sooner or later the world will look on you in
just this way. Ah well, all this was over four years
ago. Let us hope you've come along.

Have you "known" any of the local belles, behind
a hayrick or a deserted broch? In other words, are you
still a Virgin? Lord! I can't believe I am asking this of
a man nearly thirty years old! My prudent friend, "it"
will atrophy from non-use. Or fall off, leaving your
testicles with a great gaping hole above from which
you shall gush forth uncontrollably. There now. I cannot be more graphic.

I'm grateful for the detailed course of study. Lord,
I'd be home by Trinity term if I were he. Those books
can be read by such a mind without instruction, lying
on a strip of white sand, the birds wheeling and
screeching overhead, the air sweet with broom and
gorse. And you are there for the more difficult passages! Now that I muse on it (grotesque image,
"Alexander musing," what?), why is he going? No,

you will have him home within the year. Which reminds me. You say nothing about your future plans.

Have I found the love of my life? I told you, the sky will be alight with flame when and if. You know, I'll confess to you, old Robert John, for me mystery is the key to my heart. And my passions. . . . It will come! Ah, the double entendres!

Amore, Alexander

P.S. <u>Write to Isobel.</u>

The morning of his departure Michael Magnus, laird of Burrafirth, stood on the balcony of his room. He had a view of green crofts with their low stone cottages and byres, of brown peat hills, the scattalds where sheep grazed, and the purple heathered moorlands rising up behind. He saw the sea arm, his beloved firth, cutting his land into massive promontories. To his right, beyond the sandy beach, was visible the burn where he and Robert John fished and dreamed the hours away and along whose banks he gathered kingcups, laying them on the spot where his mother had sat with him that last day.

The light revealed a world of shifting color, muted yet clear. Ahead, the mist lay high and low. The stone stacks across the firth to the northeast stood like forgotten remnants of a world that had been and was no more.

Michael heard a sound behind him. It was Robert, hugging his tunic against the morning chill. Under his arm was a large bound volume.

Michael held out his hand.

"Master Robert! I wouldn't have waked you, but how glad I am you've come."

"And I would never have let you go without a last farewell. What's more, I have this for you." He put the book into Michael's hands.

"I've written down the tales and legends and myths you've favored. Keep them with you. They are," Robert said, looking away, "my thanks for all these years."

Michael swallowed hard.

"You've been my friend, as well as my tutor."

"And you, an excellent friend to me."

"Will you watch over my father? And the seals?"

"A large order," Robert answered with a smile, "but I will, young laird," and both faces were full of pleasure at the familiar expression. "Have you said your good-byes?"

"Last night. I made the rounds. All of them, Murphy and Swaabie and Jaimie. . . ." Suddenly there was a losing battle with the salt drops filling his eyes. "Why is it, with animals, it's so much harder? They don't know, I can't tell them, that I'll be back."

"It's because you've not gone before, it's harder, for you and for them. Once they see you go and you come, then, Anny says, they have their way of knowing. But look." Robert pointed northeast to the sky. It was rose satin, the sun rising directly out of the wick of Skaw.

Michael leaned on the railing.

"Is there any part of the world more beautiful?"

"I think not. To my taste there's as much beauty here as anywhere, though I've seen precious little of the world."

For moments neither spoke. Then:

"I've been thinking of Connla, Robert."

"He is in your book."

"I'm sure now that it would have been right, and *good,* the other way."

"The other way?"

"For the fairy maiden to have brought her magic into *his* world. Do you see?" Michael pointed across the firth. "A moment ago the fog curled about those stacks, they were anything I wanted them to be, anything, right here."

"Therefore?"

"Therefore not only Hercules and Achilles, born of God and woman, move between two worlds. We, too, Master Robert."

Suddenly a horn sounded, clear in the sunrise.

"Olaf is ready."

Chapter Fourteen _____

ROBERT TOOK JAIMIE onto the moors every day for the first
week after Michael's departure. The heather was pink and
purple and the tiny irregular ponds—nature's cooking ves-
sels, Anny called them—were filled with crystal-clear
water, their surfaces ridged only when a breeze blew across
from the sea.

Trotting slowly along the western ridge of Hermaness,
Robert could see the seals cavorting, though many more
than usual lay on the flat baas and, he guessed, were
grouped on the strips of beach under the steep overhang of
cliffs hidden from view. In a month there would be hun-
dreds of births!

Birth and death. What had taken the Lady Lavinia? The
scene was one of utter calm, yet he, like the others, found
himself churning within whenever he saw the seals gathered
together. Perhaps magic is not that which we don't see, but
that which lingers around the edges of our vision. Time and
again during these years he had tried to imagine her, as if
asleep, covered, no, *protected,* by the seals. Olaf had said
when they'd found her on the rock the seals had simply
slipped away into the water and disappeared. And there had
been scores of them near her. As if by a signal, Olaf had

said, all of them, on the rock and in the water, had suddenly disappeared. It was not this report alone but another that haunted Robert. Olaf had also related, no, sworn in confidence, that she had not been there the first days of their search. Nor could anyone recall whether or not the seals had been out and piled high in such numbers. It was as if a cloud had fallen across their memories.

Oh, that fateful day with Michael and Olaf! Now, were another to perpetuate such an act, his own reaction would be as was Michael's—one of outcry and, just behind it, he knew now, fear. Fear at disturbing an order. *The* order of things.

Jaimie raised his head and blew hard.

"That's right, Jaimie boy, you are part of that order. But it was shaken when the Lady Lavinia died. Or"—Robert pulled up short on the reins—"her dying was part of the order—for the seals. Lord! Can that be? Is that why they occupy so large a place in Michael's life, in his heart? What claims are theirs on our young laird."

For the next week the weather closed in. Fog made activity any distance from the house dangerous, impossible. Murphy sought consolation by Anny's side and Swaabie took over a corner of the orchard by the apple tree.

"I've told ye, creatures be no strangers to our thoughts." Anny put down her knitting. "Aye, evenin's be long without 'em both here."

Supper had been cleared away, the teatray sat ready on the kitchen table. Olaf reached into the fire with a slim long stick. When it caught, he brought it quickly and deftly to his pipe. The tobacco had a spicy odor. It was his one luxury, this quality blend he purchased in Lerwick directly from a skipper who also traded in textiles from Flanders.

"Close yur book, Robin."

Robert had tucked himself along his favorite window seat with an oil lamp beside him on Anny's workstool.

"Now the laddie's gone and ye not be teachin', least fur what I can see, I've a mind to ask ye . . ."

Olaf waved his pipe discreetly at Anny; she ignored it.

"Way back, both o' us, Olaf and myself, we were wonderin' why a bright lad like yourself comes all the way to our island?"

It was said at last, and evidently to her satisfaction, for she settled back and took up her needles, not glancing at either Olaf or Robert.

Robert swung his bare feet to the floor. The planks were surprisingly warm, like those two people sitting by the hearth. They were always surprising him and they were always warm, of heart and hand. Who ever designated "simple" for countryfolk? Anny was blatantly shrewd and Olaf, patient Viking that he appeared, was no fool.

So. They had waited until it was time, was that what Anny said? Till it was safe to ask the question, for his answer might just have upset him in the saying, sent him back to Aberdeen!

Olaf turned toward the fire, arms hugging his chest, a dark monolith in the shadows. Anny rocked and Murphy sighed and yipped through dreams of splendid hunts and glorious rewards.

There was a scratch at the window; one bright eye rested against the pane. Robert pulled on an iron handle, the glass swung open, and Swaabie flew in, lighting on Olaf's shoulder.

"Aye, it's not fur any livin' bein' to be about," Olaf said, reaching up and stroking the bird, whose own greeting was a shower of icy droplets on the man's neck.

The tea was still hot. Robert poured out three cups, two with milk and sugar, his own clear, without sweetening.

He sat down on the floor next to Anny.

"I will tell you." He was calm. He would speak of Isobel, finally.

And so he began. He began with his mother. Describing her intelligence and sweetness, her face like Eve and her voice that could always lift his mood. As he spoke the anger and hurt and feelings of betrayal poured out, so that by the time he came to Isobel and her father he realized he had been seeing his beloved as one who also had betrayed him, though she had not.

"She sounds a bonnie lass, Robin." Anny patted his shoulder. "Runnin' about the town, takin' all those chances, just to have a kiss from ye! I'd guess she's waitin' fur ye. Ye know"—she leaned across the arm of the rocker—"she wants ye to be showin' yur worth, and ye've plenty o' that, plenty!"

"Plenty!" Olaf lifted his shoulder and Swaabie squacked to a corner of the mantel. "Those letters that come to ye, time and again . . ."

"From a friend and fellow teacher at King's College."

"I'll warrant he's tellin' ye true, meanin' the same as we?"

"He does."

"Well then. . . ." Anny said.

"Well then" was Olaf's echo.

Robert placed his cup and saucer on the tray with a suddenly unsteady hand. As always just when he thought he could think of her calmly as a part of his past it all came flooding back—the humiliation and the fury . . . and the ache of deterred love.

"It's past now, Anny," he said. "Thank you for the tea. I'll be off to bed now."

"Of *course* it's past, if ye be stayin' here like a limpet on a rock, Robin lad! Ye'll not win her back by keeping silent—that bit o' magic I've yet to see!" Anny flounced out of the rocker. "No, ye best be helpin' the magic that's already come to ye, with such a love as ye have, both o' ye. . . ."

"And amen to that." Olaf pushed the stool under the table. "I'll leave the fire." He stacked three peat blocks on each side of those already glowing. "Someone be always up in the night." He added, "I've been meanin' to ask, Master Robert. No"—he grinned, the pipe expertly clenched between his teeth—"no, 'tis not another private question, but did ye notice Thomas Matheson by the seals in his boat, or seemin' to be hidin' out by the scree, when ye trotted out with Jaimie these last days?"

"God help us, Olaf, ye not be worryin' about *him* again?" Anny's eyes were closed with the thought.

"Thomas Matheson is always a menace, he is."

Robert felt the room suddenly pulsing. . . . "No, Olaf, I haven't, but then I've not been looking. What does all this mean?"

Anny shook a finger. "It best not mean what it *means*."

Olaf planted both hands on the table with a thump that sent Swaabie back to his shoulder.

"Ye know, ever since the beginnin', with the first laird o'

Burrafirth, there's been no killin' the seals, not in these waters. All the men gave in their sealin' knives. But 'tis said the Mathesons held back, though we've never found proof o' killin' all these years, but it's the *not* knowin'. Thomas now, he kills birds, and heaven knows what else, fur the sport o' it. Each year, near time fur the pups to come, I've caught him stalkin' 'round. And I *know* he's never forgotten that trouncin' give him by Michael Magnus. I know. I have him workin' fur me off 'n' on since then. He mutters he's full o' hate. So keep an eye out fur him, will ye, Robert lad? I've not mentioned this before, but with 'em both gone, I'm fearin' that man, I am. He's got respect fur Master Laurence. He knows, in his own way, it's him not wantin' to send him off the island. He knows he's still in his own cottage by the laird's grace. But when he's gone . . . I'm fearin' that man!''

Chapter Fifteen

"HE IS QUITE resplendent in his velvet cap and gown, though I decry so visible a distinction between gentleman and plebeian student."

Robert and Laurence were alone in the library after an animated supper where Olaf and Anny tumbled out question after question concerning Michael at Oxford. Satisfied that the laddie would not dematerialize without her oatcakes and stews and that his clothes would not dissolve in some alien washtub, assured that no one lurked in back wynds and mews where only he, Olaf, could protect the young laird, the two withdrew for their private evening tea.

Port in hand, Laurence moved his chair closer to the hearth.

"He was given a key to the library?" Robert fingered the cool facets of glass along the bottom of the stem, recalling that first drink they had shared six years ago.

"Yes, and he has three elegant, well-furnished rooms, complete with two servants. The English students bring their valets and the few wealthy Scotsmen likewise, but I had been advised that these rooms came with the two, jolly fellows they are, rotund and sunny, from Somerset. Willing and experienced. They'll suit, I'm sure."

"As long as there are no seals to protect, no silences to break." Robert smiled. "Yes, I know, it's an old score, long settled; but I am oddly put together, Master Laurence, I cannot seem to forget. I—"

He stopped abruptly at the look in his companion's eyes. Lord! How could he forget to whom he was speaking, a man consumed night and day by one single loss.

He quickly shifted the subject.

"And Saint John's, does it live up to its reputation as one of the most beautiful of the colleges?"

"It does. Michael's rooms are in the inner quad, the Canterbury Quad, one of the most charming and perfectly proportioned, they say, in Oxford. The arcades are Renaissance, yet they do mingle quite harmoniously. And the gardens! Robert, the gardens! Even now, green and gold in the early autumn. . . . What a splendor they must be in spring, spectacular in May and June. All in all, I am thoroughly satisfied. And so must you be, Robert John. Michael is far and away the best prepared among his classmates. He has been roundly praised by a number of dons who saw his essays and had talked with him before I left."

He slid down in his chair.

"Just entering Saint John's has raised him from boy to man—suddenly. I had not seen it before. But then . . ."

"You had not been paying that much attention in these last years, sir."

"No, I have not, and here again is something else for which I am grateful to you. You taught my son, and you loved him like a brother. Do you think . . . ?"

"Do I think he knows *you* love him? Yes, but I must say you have missed good years. Nonetheless it can be rectified; I can attest to it, he loves you. You must not chide yourself, there is time to change."

"Time?" Laurence closed his eyes. "There was a moment in my life when youth in its most lush bloomed by my side and I thought, There is world enough and time enough. You know the rest. This is not so, Robert John."

Laurence fell soon after into a deep slumber. Robert tiptoed out of the room. These naps overtook the man often now. Besides, Robert was sure, the trip had been a long one and, there was no doubt, had drained his emotions as well as his body.

Give heed, Robert John.

He closed the door softly.

How much time indeed? How much?

Mid-December
Oxford

Pace to all!

Do you realize, this is the first letter I have ever written? What a comment on the extent of my travel experiences! Don't feel badly, Father. I never wished myself anywhere but Burrafirth, and now I discover that I have been happier there than I knew, which *is* the way, isn't it?

I shall pretend we are all sitting round the kitchen table. Anny has made a pot of her "choice" tea, Olaf's pipe is puffing away (I can smell the aroma!), Robert has closed the breviary he always carries. Father, I'm not sure about. What would you be doing? Well, you'd be there, which is what matters! Murphy by the hearth, Swaabie on the mantel, Jaimie in his stall with plenty of hay, for I know it's been a good *haist*—there, Anny! I shall never give up the uld ways!

Now I've just described a scene most unlikely to be found in this city of spires and weathered stone.

You were right, Father. Tim and Jones serve me with affection and enjoy their jobs. They're very curious about life in Shetland and I've been painting vivid pictures for them! For that matter, everyone is curious. I can't imagine what they expected but the Scots *are* despised at Westminster and hence everywhere else. No, let me revise that rather extreme interpretation. If not despised, then disdained, which can be nearly as devastating, for does not the Bible somewhere say that to humiliate a man is to murder him?

They're a rare mix, my classmates. The rich ones are, on the whole, feckless and lazy, even when they are intelligent (more's the crime, you say, Robert? Right!). The poorer ones one hardly sees, for they are studying! There is a description of an undergraduate life written this year in the *Oxford Sausage*. I can't do better myself than record it here for you. I add immediately, this is *not* my life nor the life of my few friends:

I Rise about nine, get to Breakfast by ten,
Blow a Tine on my Flute, or perhaps make a Pen;
Read a Play till eleven, or cork my lac'd Hat;
Then step to my Neighbors, till Dinner, to chat.
Dinner over, to Tom's or to Jame's I go.
The News of the Town so impatient to know;
While Law, Locke, and Newton, and all the rum Race,
That talk of their Modes, their Ellipses, and Space,
The Seat of the Soul, and new Systems on high,

In Holes, as abstruse as their Mysteries lie.
From the Coffee House then I to Tennis away,
And at five I post back to my College to pray.
I sup before eight and secure from all Duns,
Undauntedly march to the Mitre or Tuns; [pubs,
which I *do* frequent!]
Where in Punch or good Claret [not as good as
yours, Father!] my Sorrows I drown,
And toss off a Bowl 'To the best in the Town';
At one in the morning, I call what's to pay,
Then Home to my College I stagger away.
Thus I tope all the Night, as I trifle all Day.

''The Seat of the Soul,'' yes, I should be overjoyed
to have revealed, but it shan't be here, in this city of
Spires and layabeds!

My tutor is a Don named David Collins. Languages
are his specialty, which is why, I am sure, I have been
assigned to him—or rather, he has been assigned
to me. Which perspective one chooses has a great
deal, I am convinced, to do with the success or fail-
ure of the relationship! Is it to be believed, Robert,
there are tutors and students who are strangers
to each other? This man, Collins, is most intelligent and they say in form and manner resembles Mr.
David Hume (as a young man, though Mr. Collins
must be near 40!). He is very rotund with an enormous head and eyes set at a deep slant under bristle
brows.

Here is MY DAY!

Rise at Dawn.

Pray (in Latin) with my peers in the Quad.
Walk.
Breakfast   8 A.M.
Philosophy   9 A.M.
Minor Prophets!   10 A.M.
To the coffee House where we Discuss 11 A.M.
Mr. David Collins   1 P.M. We have started
  reading Aristotle's *Rhetoric* (me, for the sec-
  ond time; he cannot fathom this).
Punting   This will be moved up, as it is al-
  ' ready too dark at 4 P.M. for such excursions!
Dinner   6 P.M.
Read Horace or Ovid or Catullus (yes, Father
  and Robert, I am now grown-up!).
Be Sociable!
Prayers   10 P.M.

In the morning I pray for an uneventful day and in
the evening I give thanks for this having come to
pass.
   I am going into Buckinghamshire with a friend for
the Holidays. I shall miss the festivities at Home!
   Father, don't be surprised if I am home long before
the term of study expires.

Your *filius amans*

P.S. Anny, Mr. Collins says that words have the true
power. I told him everyone on Shetland knows this!

   Michael quickly became a favorite at Oxford, giving the
lie to the notion that all Scots were rough and those from the

islands no more than boors—though his new friends wondered at how unexpectedly he might withdraw into himself, his eyes on something far beyond the walls. At the beginning of Trinity term, in spring, he sat with his friends in the paneled Common Hall. The wine in their goblets was, he said, the color of his cliffs and the pale crystal a million points of light like his firth.

"And your woman, Michael Magnus, what is your woman like?" An elegantly dressed student nearer twenty years old leaned back, admiring his own impeccably booted foot.

"My *woman?*" The tips of Michael's ears began to burn. Strange, he had been asked that question by a jocund Tim just a few days before.

"The girls, Master Magnus, or girl you've left behind, lad. You've not said a word of them. Aye, you've won your share, we've no doubt. Young as you be, there's a special one among 'em, eh? What of her?

"You see," his perfectly shod friend continued, "we've all decided, since we know how you admire beauty, we have been together at those boring garden parties, Lord knows, but since you never accompany us on our little *excursions,* 'Derek,' I say to myself, 'he has a love at home.'" And the speaker peered at Michael, his goblet to one eye like a quizzing glass.

The others smiled. Derek was a tease, but the tone was far from jest. What *was* the key, they had been asking themselves these months, to this young aristocrat from the north?

A love at home? Michael looked around at his friends, some lounging carelessly in immense chairs of rough-cut velvet, others on the floor, lush cushions supporting their elbows. Pleasant chaps, good-natured, intelligent. But he had seen their loves, if loves they were. He had caught glimpses of them behind hastily latched doors, overdressed, overpainted, behind a shutter blown open by a sudden wind, or exposed by a shaft of light within a darkened wynd or close. He had once walked past such women on the street. Their odor reminded him of rotting stems disintegrating, a flowery but stagnant, acrid smell.

A love at home! And as the old ache was bearing down in his chest he sensed an exhilaration, a glory. Of course! A love at home!

Gripping his fingers around the cool stem, he raised the goblet. "Yes, Derek, to my love at home!" His racing heart cried out: "To my firth." Though the last was given as part of the toast, there was an insistence in his voice that caused the others to hesitate before joining him. Then, crystal touched.

"To the laird of the North. To his firth."

Derek pirouetted to the center of the room. "And to his love at home."

Michael let the sweet dark port flow slowly down his throat. Then abruptly he was on his feet. He nodded to the company and left the room.

No one said a word as the door shut behind him.

Finally a slim towheaded youth tossed his cushion into the air, catching it on two fingers above his head.

"You know him better than any of us, Derek; he spent Noël with you. Did we offend him? God knows, it wasn't my intention or any of ours, right?" He looked around at the others, who all nodded in agreement.

Derek refilled his glass and passed the decanter to his companion.

"No, good heavens. He was probably thinking of 'her.' He knows we mean him no harm. He drank to that firth of his but his mind was elsewhere."

Mid-July
Oxford

Pater Pace,
I am coming home.
Michael Magnus, young laird of
Burrafirth.

Two month later his carriage approached the ness. It was twilight of a golden September day. The firth was amethyst. A salty freshness was blowing in from the sea.
"I shall *not* leave again."

Chapter Sixteen _____

"IT WAS A broken heart took him, Olaf."

Anny stood with the skipper looking out at Bluemull Sound. The isolated headland glistened in the sunlight from the mica studding its surface. Behind them, Michael's back was to the view as he stood beside his father's grave close to his mother's headstone. Robert John was a few yards away.

"When there's no end to grief the body can't take it, never mind the heart. He told me, more 'n once, he'd an ache in there every minute o' every day. Ye can't be livin' so. There weren't no sickness, you heard the doctor. He just went off. He went to her." Anny sought Olaf's hand and the two who had known Laurence from the moment of his birth, and his parents before that, looked at each other, their faces a wash of tears.

"Aye, and here we are, dusty, with time still goin' on. Aye, he's been part dead since she went, it be true. And I've been thinkin', he was waitin' till the laddie was ready. He's laird now, is Michael Magnus. Just the sight o' that lad would turn anyone right, but no, Master Laurie was waitin'."

Anny pulled Olaf farther away, to a low stone wall surrounding the cemetery.

"Sit down, Olaf. And keep yur voice a whisper. He was seein' *her* in the laddie more 'n' more. There's no grievin' away someone livin', ye can't say dead and buried when the one be walkin' and talkin' and laughin' in front o' yur eyes, can ye now? It were a terrible thing fur him all these years. But there weren't a cure fur it, no more'n there was fur her, Lord love 'em."

"Master Robert." Michael's voice covered Anny's last words.

Robert came up quickly to Michael's side. A strained face looked down on him but there were no tears.

"Are your parents lying side by side?"

Robert felt a coating of dust on his tongue. He nodded yes.

"It's all right this way." Michael touched the marble slab. "Anny came to my room last night. She wanted me to know that the love my parents had for each other was so great, she said, it could only be an expression of God's mercy and love. It was a gift from Him. She said I should think of them joyful, side by side, *and* in Heaven."

Michael took Robert's arm, leading him from the small burial ground to the shoulder of the hill.

"It must be wonderful and terrible to have such a love. I always knew, even as a small boy, that my father was a sad man. And nothing I did filled the gap. I always knew I could not make him happy. I tried, oh, how I tried! If only he might have felt even a little, as I did, as I do. She is always with me, Robert. May I call you Robert?"

"Absolutely—Michael."

Michael was insistent.

"What were your feelings about your mother?"

The old sense of Michael's hitting dead center in matters of the heart pierced Robert like an arrow to its mark.

"My mother is everywhere, Robert. Everywhere. And when I was at Saint John's, it was the same. Did I ever tell you that they asked me did I have a love at home? I answered yes. . . ." His voice trailed off as he turned toward the freshly mounded grave.

"I said yes."

Michael ran a hand through his hair, a gesture so reminiscent, to Robert, of Laurence.

"I think we'd best go home. Come, we'll round up Anny and Olaf and be off. There's work to be done. Olaf!"

The voice has changed. Overnight. He surely will have a love someday. And he will not hesitate . . . Robert didn't let himself finish the thought.

Hearing the call, Olaf pulled Anny up from the wall. He straightened his jacket and helped her brush bits of earth and moss from her skirt.

"Come on, Anny, there's the laird hailin' us. And I'm thinkin' the call has a new fine ring to it. Just what we'll be needin', just. . . ."

The earth settled over Laurence's grave and a calm settled over the household at the Ness.

Michael entered into the routine enthusiastically. With Anny he visited the crofters and fishermen, with Robert he spent hours poring over the accounts, answering letters from his solicitors in Lerwick and Aberdeen, and becoming generally familiar with the running of the estate. He continued the tradition of his family, a tradition dating back to the first lairds of Burrafirth. What was reasonable, not a hardship, was collected from each family in rent. Nothing was taken in time of spare harvest or poor catch or sickness.

One late afternoon Michael and Robert climbed to their spot above the firth. The moor was a carpet of pink and purple, the delicate bell-like flowers just beginning to go by.

"Look here, Mas . . . Robert." Michael was still having trouble, or, as Anny put it, the old way was still on his tongue. "Look here." He held out a purple flower with petals stretching from a center like angels' wings. "The hedge woundwort," he said, laughing. "Incredibly ugly name for so lovely a creation. Have you noticed it's covering all the derelict ground by the roadside? It really doesn't belong here; its home is in the south of France, but it's come. Feel it." He stroked the pale-blue corolla, with its arched upper lip and spreading lower blossom.

Robert fingered the satin finish.

Michael, who was just establishing himself comfortably on the ground, suddenly shot up to the edge of the cliff.

"In the middle of the firth, just above the water, there's something there, like smoke whirling or . . ."

He cupped his hands around his eyes.

Robert moved closer.

"A haze, I'd say, but there are splashes rising. Strange. . . ."

With the sun going down behind them, the water was a mirror for the opposite cliffs. Whatever it was, it hung over the surface then, funnellike, was drawn under, leaving a tiny whirlpool behind.

Michael's foot was nearly over the edge.

"Where did it go, Robert? It's gone now. Where is it?" He took hold of Robert's arm in a hard grip.

"Where is it?"

"Gently there, young laird, gently. *What* is it, is more the question, is it not? I've never seen any animal activity this far into the firth. Near the mouth, yes, but . . . What do you think, Michael Magnus?"

Michael's answer came swiftly.

"For what I think, Robert John, you would laugh me off this cliff. Yes indeed you would. And . . . My God! Look! It's come up beneath us; look, Robert." For the haze had suddenly reorganized itself into a slim white arrow of smoke directly below them. And then, as suddenly as it had come, it was gone, not dispersing but disappearing.

Robert put up a hand to Michael's shoulder. In a gesture totally alien, Michael moved away so that the hand meant to comfort fell across his body and down, away. All this was accompanied by a shudder, causing Robert to step back.

Michael stood alone. He was taken with a suffocating desire to be alone. He could feel, without turning, he had hurt his friend.

"Forgive me" was on his tongue, but he could not say it.

Any word would be shattering. He wanted silence and he wanted suddenly to be alone.

Twilight had melted into night as the two stood, each shrouded in his own thoughts. The moon, three-quarters full, cast a blinding whiteness beaming onto the spot where the haze had been. A faint circle was on the water.

Michael turned, stopped a moment by Robert's side, then walked away slowly across the moor.

Robert stood watching the water absorb the moon.

For no reason, the words he had heard the young laird whisper chilled him.

It is time.

* * *

Michael rose at six, in darkness, for by the end of October the day had shrunk nearly to its winter size. He was exhilarated, though he had barely slept. As he had lain under the covers he was sure that Robert, too, had been wakeful, deep under the quilt whose intriguing pattern he used to trace with a finger. Nothing to be done now. He would see him on his return.

At the firth, with Murphy and a lantern at his feet, Michael stood in the early-morning chill. Nothing stirred; the birds still slept. Slowly the first dawn light broke over Saxavord, out of the bay of Skaw, and still nothing moved. Only the sky was agitated, menacing clouds were overhead. When the cold mist began rolling in, Michael waved his cloak closer about him, secured it with the gold trefoil, and headed home.

Robert heard Michael leave. He swung out of bed soon after, dejected, an alien feeling in these last years, though before he had come to Unst it had been too often with him.

After a cold wash, dressed in fresh linen, Robert came down the stairs. There was activity in the dining room. Laurence had always enjoyed a leisurely morning meal—in the style of the mainland, he would comment wryly—and this was being continued. The table was laid on a snowy cloth, with the crystal and china and silver that the Lady Lavinia had brought with her from Edinburgh. Anny was just covering a plate of pork chops sizzling in its frypan.

She looked up.

"I heard you— Lord, Master Robin, ye're the color o' rainclouds. Be ye feelin' poorly, lad?"

Her hand was on the tea cozy and the next moment Robert was holding a cup of her strong brew.

"Sit." Anny fairly pushed Robert into his chair. "He's gone out, the laddie has."

"We saw a haze on the water, late afternoon, yesterday. Moving about *so* strangely, Anny." Robert drained his cup. "What does it mean? It almost took Michael straight off the cliff. That's it!" Robert shook his head in utter bewilderment. "Straight off the cliff. He was gone from my side, for all the while he was there in the flesh. Anny?"

Anny refilled his cup. Then she poured some tea into a saucer and brought it carefully to her lips. Her eyes half closed as she blew on the liquid.

"A haze 'twas what ye saw?"

Robert nodded.

She continued blowing. Then a sharp tilt upward and the tea was gone. Anny placed the saucer on the table beside the teapot and rested her hands in her lap.

"Well then, Master Robin, we'll wait, we will."

"Wait for *what,* Anny?"

"For whatever it is, this haze," was the matter-of-fact reply. Then, seeing his face pained and anxious, Anny added:

"Look here, Robin lad. There was somethin' and it spoke to the laddie, so strong it was fur him it fair took him—or his spirit!—from right off beside ye. Well, we'd best stay close by him, then, and wait. If it's come, then it's time it's come. And we'd best be near."

In the library Robert sat behind the massive table—flesh-wood, Olaf called it. Three bulging ledgers lay before him, closed. After his conversation with Anny he'd walked around the house, offered a chunk of bread to Swaabie, then returned, unable to shake his malaise. Now he was scraping the point of a quill pen to an unnecessary sharpness. It was a thing to do, without concentrating. The fire was bright and the room familiar and elegant. Yet he felt chilled, miserable.

He looked up as Michael entered.

He has grown as tall and comely as Connla. Connla! Connla had left, but Michael . . . And Robert felt some of the misery lift, the stone in the pit of his stomach loosed. Michael had reacted violently against the leaving. Michael had said the fairy maiden should have stayed, brought the magic to the land. . . . But what had all this to do with a haze on the firth? Why was he thinking along these lines?

"Robert." Michael stood close to the table, hands fiddling with the gold trefoil on his shoulder. "Do let me explain."

Robert laid aside the pen. "First, sit down, young laird." A faint smile came to his lips. "And stop playing with the brooch. Anny tightened the catch just yesterday and if it comes off, we'll both be trounced!"

The image of Anny exercising her high-handedness brought a light to both their faces and immediately the old ease was back between them. Michael sat down in the broad high-backed chair that had been his father's favorite.

"What can I say? I feel as if I am on fire, quite simply on fire! Every fiber in me is screaming—I don't know why, I've never felt this way." He stopped.

Robert folded his hands on one of the volumes.

He'll ask me next, Have I ever been on fire? And what will I answer? That for me dreams must suffice, and so I have chosen that route? A route surely not for him, no, not for the laird of Burrafirth.

"You do understand, Robert; I *know* you do. I have to go about it alone. I feel this. I can't tell you why."

Robert got up and came around to Michael, who was on his feet instantly.

"No!" The younger man smiled. "Don't reproach me for standing. I will never be otherwise from the days when it was *de rigueur* for me to stand. Just tell me you have a sense of what I am feeling. That's all I need. As a friend, as a man, tell me you understand, and that you are not hurt. By my sharpness last night."

"I understand and I am not hurt. Go. . . ." Robert took Michael's hands in his. "Your hands are cold."

"So are yours. Dear friend. . . ."

"Go. Go the route that is yours, the road I have yet to travel. I am here. We are here. We are all here. Go."

Anny, in the kitchen, saw Michael leave. She put down the potato with the peel still hanging, wiped her hands on her apron, and ran out the door.

"Laddie!"

Michael turned and Murphy, who had been waiting by the stone wall, bounded back toward the woman. She swept across the turf.

"Michael lad, Master Robin's a bit troubled, he is."

She squinted. The onions she had been chopping had watered her eyes.

"What was it ye think ye saw, laddie? Ye can tell Anny. Come here, sit."

They both sat down on the wall.

"Are ye feverish, Michael?" She put a hand to his cheek

and forehead. "Ye be hot but ye be shiverin'. What is it, lad?"

"Anny!"

She drew Michael to her as she had done unaccountable times to him, and to his father before, but this time Michael pulled away.

"No, Anny, it's not that. I've not scraped my knee, nor am I weeping for Mother, nor have I found a lamb drowned off the cliff. I've been waiting, *you* know this. I think it's here. It's a feel, you've told me so often, it's a *feel*. 'Don't point that knife,' you'd say, 'you might cut something in the air, something in the invisible world.' I saw it yesterday, Anny. I know I did!"

Michael was breathing quickly, his eyes bright, not with tears but with fire, with the waiting and the coming.

"I know I did."

"Aye, I'm sure ye did. But it's givin' ye a turn. I'm understandin' this but get hold, laddie. If it's there, then it's not going anywhere. That's what I told Robin, that's what I'm tellin' ye," and she brushed off some imaginary dust from his shoulders.

"What did Robert say?"

"'Twas at breakfast, just after ye'd gone. He saw ye be no mite taken with it, this haze. He was worried, he was. I'm thinkin' now what yur father'd be sayin'."

"What would Father say?"

The air, full of mist, had matted Michael's hair to his temples. Anny saw him across the years, coming to her after a fall or with a dead chick in hand.

"What would Master Laurie say? Oh, laddie, I'd be hopin' he'd say, 'If it's come, it's meant, and we'd best be together, clingin'.' That's the thing now, laddie."

"He did say that, Anny. To me, years ago. So now I'm going out onto the firth. Alone. I've got to go alone. I told that to Robert. *You* see this, don't you?"

"No explainin' to me, Michael Magnus. I see, that's just what I do, and so does Master Robin—now. I'm simply statin', we're all here. That's all. It's fur ye to go."

They stood up.

"My, ye be tall! Here, bend down, and I'll send ye off proper."

Noticing the flush come into his face, Anny clucked.

"Yes, I know, ye be a grown man and—"

Michael stopped her with a kiss on one cheek and was gone.

Anny walked slowly back to the house. Murphy followed on her heels.

"Aye, Murphy dog, ye be feelin' somethin', too. Come on, then, we'll get a plate o' breakfast on the table fur Olaf."

She could see Michael making his way below to the boats. And she remembered another time, another boy. . . .

"Oh, Master Laurie." The knot in her chest drove the words hard within her. "What *would* ye be sayin'? What would *she* be sayin', now it's come?"

Chapter Seventeen _____

THE BOATHOUSE WAS just by the sandy beach that marked the south end of the firth.

The stable was there, also. Michael stopped to pet Jaimie. The pony nuzzled against him. Jaimie had been the hardest to leave when he went away to school. And it was clear from Jaimie's way, each time he was with Michael, the animal was not yet sure his master was back to stay.

"Don't be givin' him a sweet, my laird." A bent old man came from the shadow of the stable. His eyes were like amber beads, his skin sallow. "When ye were a lad ye were always sneakin' a bit o' sweet into his mouth."

"I've come for a boat today, Ivar."

"Will ye be goin' far, my laird?"

"North to the end of the firth, up one side and down the other."

Michael had scoured every cave and grotto in his head through the night, till he had felt his eyes about to pop.

Ivar called out, "Edward!" and an awkward freckled boy of about eleven came running up.

"Get the new boat ready for the laird, the one with the wide ribs, that Olaf pulled in yesterday. Have ye a moment, my laird?"

Michael knew Ivar loved a chat but the rapid beating of his heart that had begun as he neared the water made talking impossible. He was too impatient to be gone.

"Another time, Ivar. I'd better—"

"I'd better be tellin' ye somethin.'" Ivar rubbed a grimy hand over his nose. "We're in a rumble here. This lad"— he pointed to Edward, who was struggling with the oarlocks—"was runnin' about Suther's Fields yesterday and he swears"—Ivar raised a menacing finger—"he swears, near twilight, he seen a thin flittin' about in the water."

"It's *truth*." The boy's voice was shrill.

Ivar shot out an arm. "Speak with respect before the laird!"

Michael felt what little breath he had leave him. He went over to the boy. The weakness was back in his legs. When he spoke, it was a whisper.

"What is truth, young fellow?"

"I seen a thin . . . Sir, I seen it. Swimmin' the water as if it were born to it. All light-like, the water was, and then the fog come over it, but before that I seen it. Thomas Matheson, he was there, too. Crouchin' he was, behind a stack o' peat. Black hair with kelp in it and—"

"That'll be enough," Ivar bellowed out. "Can't ye see the blood's pulled from the laird's face just with the idea o' this tale o' yurs?" And he pushed a trembling Edward aside, setting the oarlocks straight himself. "Don't be mindin' him, my laird. He's full o' tales, that one is. Go yur way, enjoy the firth. 'Tis another glory today. Here, I'll help ye in."

Michael headed north. The water was covered with black

guillemots, common gulls, and a solitary gannet that should have gone south to its winter home.

"Which of you saw?"

The words caressed the air as sleek heads dipped and shook.

"Who knows?" Michael asked louder and the birds alighted, touching down ahead of the boat.

"What *is* it?" he dared not ask.

He dipped the oars with short, angled strokes. A few minutes of steady rowing and he was, he judged, at the spot. He looked to his left. Across was the cave that held a memory he would carry not just for his life, but beyond the grave, if this could be. It was there, the day before his mother died, that he had seen, for the first time, the red-necked phalarope.

"For luck," Laurence had called them, pulling in the oars and taking Michael on his lap.

Father!

Michael closed his eyes. The early-morning mist had risen but the sky was dark and a fine rain was coming down. He floated with the boat, in it, yet himself floating.

Suddenly the boat rocked. Michael opened his eyes. Not a ripple disturbed the water's surface. Yet the boat had rocked or been rocked. Rocked as surely as one takes hold and rocks a cradle.

He dropped to his knees, thrusting an oar, carefully, far into the water. The water came over his shoulder to the neck. Back and forth against the natural pressure of the water he moved the oar all around the boat. Nothing.

"Nothing!" Michael blew out his breath and drew in his chin, biting his lower lip.

Helped by a west wind, the current had carried the boat across the firth, not far from the cave. Pond weed lay across the entrance, its thin green spikes leaning into the breeze. On this side of the firth opposite and beyond the Ness the cliffs were extremely rugged, sharp, with jutting overhangs.

Michael guided the boat through the opening. A salty odor filled his nostrils. Cold, wet air hit his face as he drew in the oars. It was two or three minutes before his eyes grew accustomed to the darkness.

The rock porphyry glistened. Small stalactites hung from the rood. What stunning color there had been when his father had brought in a torch to show him the cryptlike cathedral ceiling. On the wall, he remembered, the bosses had been deep purple.

"Hallo." Michael couldn't resist a call.

Halloo. The echo made its way back, sending two rock doves from off their nest somewhere in the blackness.

Michael gave a shove with the oar and the small craft was again outside the mouth of the cave.

One cave. Two rock doves. No phalaropes. Nothing.

Entering the house after Michael had left her, Anny stopped by the study, knocked softly, then opened the door.

Robert was sitting in the chair vacated by Michael.

"I saw him, Master Robin. He'll be all right."

She came over to him, all warmth and comfort.

"He's grown now, fur all he looks like a boy. But he's sixteen this month, aye, and a grand young man, fur the thoughts he has in his head now, book thoughts, that is." Robert couldn't help smiling at her effort to "put it all right," as she would conclude herself. "Aye, the year passed and we've been busy, as ye said. Why, ye've some grey in the beard and about the ears, ye have!''

"He's gone out onto the firth, has he?''

"Aye.''

"What will he find, Anny?''

"There's no tellin', Robin lad.''

"But he'll find something. . . .''

"Aye, somethin'. Aye.''

On his return Michael said nothing. Olaf was by the beach mending a net with Ivar, both in close conversation. He wouldn't bother the skipper with the mad ways of Thomas Matheson; if what Edward said was true, there was time to deal with it. But deal with it he would. He had never forgotten the goldcrest, and was he not now laird of Burrafirth?

Michael said nothing the next day or the following days and weeks. Daily he took out the boat and rowed the firth around and across, across and around and along. He drifted close to the stacks. He sat in the middle of the boat and waited for the rocking to begin again. Nothing.

He said nothing and nothing was said to him.

Robert watched and tried to stay busy.

Anny watched and took to wearing a molucca bean around her neck.

Olaf sat by the sandy beach and kept a weather eye out for Thomas Matheson, whose cottage was not far off. Olaf came each day, offering his services to Ivar.

Then, one grey November morning, Michael was inexplicably pressed to row past the tip of Hermaness and south again toward the seals. None were out. The rocks lay naked, a random pitch by some giant wading through the sea. When he thought about it later it had not been a conscious decision. It had been as if unseen hands were pulling the oars.

He rowed on. Suddenly his right oar refused to move. It was being pulled to a vertical position and from beneath the water came a high sweet laugh.

The girl eased herself over the side of the boat, her naked body covered with droplets shimmering on her glossy skin. When she finally spoke to him her voice was low with a slight huskiness behind it.

"I'm here," she said.

How could he answer? He could only stare.

"Michael *Magnus!*" The girl dipped her hand into the water and splashed him energetically. "I'm *here!*"

The water hit Michael squarely in the eyes. Only in books and paintings in Oxford had he seen a woman's naked body. In dreams and just before sleep he had woven his own fancies; he was struck dumb by how wide of the mark had been his night companions.

She was looking at him, her round eyes watchful, slightly amused. From her oval face Michael's gaze came to rest on her small, lithe body. Her legs were drawn together, emphasizing the dark triangle where each curl, like the curls on her forehead and neck, carried a minute bit of the sea. There was nothing of his own trembling astonishment in her demeanor as she sat before him.

"If you would, please, you might give me your cloak," she said quietly.

Who is this that cometh up from the wilderness?

Her breasts were like two pomegranates but they were also apple halves, shining pink, the nipples indented. His hands ached to touch them. She was standing by him, head to one side, saying again, "You might give me your cloak, Michael Magnus, if it makes you easier."

And bending over him she loosed the gold catch, letting the wrap fall from his shoulders. His face came up against her neck where one strand of hair lay dripping still. Michael parted his lips. Brine and the taste of lavender filled his mouth and rose like smoke to his nostrils, burning and caressing him.

"Aude." She just managed the name as his kisses were on her lips, her face, her hair and neck and breasts, then back again to her mouth. "My name is Aude."

A moment later the rains came and the boat rocked as the waves hit in short violent heaves against its sides.

Above, the gulls screeched, dipping and rising, rising and dipping, but neither one in the boat saw or heard.

When they finally moved apart, spent and hushed, Aude laid a hand on Michael's cheek. Her smile was brilliant, a loving triumph in her eyes.

"My love. My Aude! I've been waiting, I've—"

A finger was on his lips.

"I, too, my love; I, too."

Chapter Eighteen _____

AT EACH END OF the boat a lantern threw out its oily light. The rain had ceased, the sky was closed in, dark. Opposite Michael, Aude sat nearly lost in his wrap, her face a third light in the quickening darkness. Not a word had passed between them after her finger had touched his lips. The oars had idled on the choppy water, then finally Michael had begun to row, first casually, then with a fury to match the crosscurrents fighting his strokes.

Now they were in the firth. Aude stretched within the vastness of the cloak.

Michael looked at her. She had twisted her hair into a high knot, fastening it with a leather thong from his pocket.

A love at home. At home.

He let the words ring in his head, pound his temples as the water was pounding the boat. Shiver after shiver went through him, but not from cold and not from fear. She was here. She was sitting before him. And it was November of his sixteenth year with night falling by midafternoon.

There was no doubt that one could be sick with joy. She was his love. Was he not to the mark, watching his fellow Oxonians and assuring himself again and again:

"I have seen their loves and I shall know mine. . . ."

"Michael?"

"No talking, my love. I'll need all my strength to get us . . ." He hesitated, his face a pride of radiance. "To get us home."

Securing the boat at the Ness, Michael lifted Aude in his arms. She was light against his tunic. One curl had again strayed to her neck and he let his tongue suck up the last salty drops.

A moment later, arrow straight, she was standing beside him.

They threaded along the path, her hand in his. A break in the clouds revealed myriad stars; moonlight flooded the ground.

"What will they think?"

"They, my own?"

Her fingers curled tightly, the nails sharp into his knuckles.

"Anny and Olaf and Robert John. And Jaimie and Swaabie and Murphy."

Michael swung in front of her, amazement as clear as moonlight on his face.

"You know their names!"

She nodded and smiled, revealing a row of small, perfectly set teeth.

"And yours, did I not? Why so amazed?" And again her finger to his lips.

"Mine! Of course." He heard the laughing "Michael Magnus, I'm here," as she'd climbed into the boat. No, he had not been startled, not by that. Nor had she expected it otherwise, had she?

"You know everything!"

"Not *everything,* sweetheart." Aude's arms barely

reached his neck and had there been more light he would
have seen the blush heat her cheeks. "But I do know the
names of those who love you. Laurence and Lavinia. I have
to, don't I?" She lingered on the last two names.

As if to leave time for an answer, Michael began tracing
the line from her high forehead down the long slim nose to
her lips, full and moist. It was a beautiful face but possessed
of far more than beauty; and because of this, he would never
have enough of it. No, no one would ever tire of a face of
such intelligence and mischief. On the contrary . . . And
again his heart was banging in his breast.

They walked silently. Aude stretched out Michael's arm,
drawing it about her waist and bringing his hand to cup over
the breast within the cloak.

What could he expect from them whose names she knew?

Anny and Olaf he had known a lifetime; Robert, it
seemed also, forever. Yet right now he felt bereft of any
clue. How would they react, this family of his?

A turn in the path and light appeared in the great shadow
of the house.

"Aude?"

"Michael?"

"Nothing."

"It will be all right."

Her breast moved with her breath and the dimpled nipple
again grew hard under his touch.

There was no place for him but at her side. Whatever the
others thought or said or did.

The lamps along the wall of the staircase and corridor had
been lit earlier in the day. Anny led Aude upstairs.

When ye're waitin', ye're surprised but ye're not sur-prised. Lord help us. The thought lay unspoken in her heart.

There had been enough amazement in that kitchen when the girl had walked in with Michael behind to take care of a lifetime of surprises. What did those two, Olaf and Robin, think the last weeks had been all about? She'd seen their faces during the tea drunk in silence, and gotten Aude away quickly, coming around to the girl like a bastion against trouble. And the young ones, like a pair of frightened lambs, looking from Olaf to Robin and back to her. . . .

Had the girl wanted to say something to Robert? Anny wondered now, watching Aude take each step on tiptoe, slowly, with an intense look, as if concentrating on a wholly new skill. Aye, for a moment by the kitchen table it had looked as if she'd been about to speak, but then Michael had caught Anny's eye and here they were, almost to the first landing.

"Aye, ye're tired, child, extra tired. And about to freeze," she added, looking down at Aude's bare feet. "And there's nothin' on under that wrap, I'll warrant?"

Aude shook her head. "I am cold, Anny. And tired. I'm *so* tired. I've come so far and—"

"And I'll get ye to bed with a hot grog in yur belly. Tomorrow we'll see to it all, child. Tomorrow." She started up the last short flight, Aude following with a surer tread. At the end of the corridor Anny chose a key from the cluttered ring hanging at her waist and opened the door in front of them. "'Tis the laddie's old nursery. There a fine warm bed. I'll be happy havin' it used again, I will. Come, child." Anny pulled the curtains aside. "In the mornin' ye be havin' a grand look at the firth. I'll get ye some clothes and we'll have Olaf start up a fire. Ye be climbin' into the bed while I'm about my business.''

"Anny . . . thank you."

"Ye're *welcome,* Aude child. Ye're *welcome* in this house," the old woman said and she pulled the door closed.

Aude sat down on the bed. The light through the window was as bright as the light that had lit her way here. But her thoughts were not with the house or the others. They were with the young man sitting in the kitchen, and with her love for him that was even now washing over her like the ebb and flow of tide, leaving her at once secure and vulnerable, joyous and very near to tears, alone and yet, for the first time in her short life, totally a part of someone else.

She stretched and the cloak fell from her body. The moonlight emphasized the down, grey-gold, covering her skin.

Lying back, her arms moved in circles above her head. Then she rolled over and buried her face in the pillows.

"Eiders," she whispered, and with a half smile playing about her eyes, she crawled under the puff.

Once outside the room Anny almost dragged herself down the hallway to a door directly opposite the nursery. The familiar voices floated up from below.

"They'll be askin' him who she is, they will," she said to herself, and the woman's body shook. "We *know* who she is, Lord o' Heaven. It was writ who she is. She's the laddie's chosen, and that's it, isn't it?" The last words were sputtered out at invisible assailants. Then she recalled her errand and with a great sigh opened the door of Laurence's room for the first time since the funeral.

A chest close by the bed was covered with a large, light

lap shawl. Another sigh came from her bosom and she brought the molucca bean to her lips. Then she knelt, whipped off the shawl, and lifted the lid.

A heavy lingering smell of lavender rose up as layer after layer of clothing was exposed.

"Oh, my lady, oh, I know they'll fit, though she be shorter. Oh, but she's boned as you were. Oh, lady, what *am* I doin', what?"

Anny fumbled about until she came on a dark-blue linsey-woolsey. With this on her arm she pulled out a shift, a petticoat, and a pair of stockings, dropped the lid, and was out the door.

"There now, 'tis *done!* She's got to be dressed!"

Anny, torn with the demands of the moment and her fervent desire to leave memories intact, stood outside the room and wept. Then, wiping her face on a corner of the petticoat, she took down a lamp from the wall and walked briskly to the nursery where Aude lay asleep.

Laying the garments on the end of the bed, Anny shuffled out. She leaned against the closed door with the weariness of one whose bones had grown suddenly heavy. Then, as if hoisting herself from within, she took a deep breath, straightened up, patted the sides of her hair, and headed downstairs.

There was a long silence after the two women left. Olaf busied himself stoking the fire to its hottest and replaced the kettle on the hob to boil up for another pot of tea. Michael took Aude's cup and drank the remains. It was cold and bitter, but the salty taste of her mouth on its rim made his head swim.

Cross-legged before the fire, he scanned the faces of the two men standing at each end of the mantel.

How much shall I tell them? How much need I tell them? How much do I know, intellectually know?

The fire hissed an answer, but no one was speaking. Slowly the kettle sent out a swell of steam from its long half hoop of a spout. In a corner Murphy shifted positions and grunted out from his puppy years far back in dreams.

Robert pulled nervously at his beard.

Why had he not come forward when the girl entered? His reticence had not been worthy of the utter joy he'd read on Michael's face, joy and nervous anticipation. Unworthy! The word stung like a birch switch. As unworthy as Lord Eglinton had found him, as unworthy as had been his outburst at the seals long ago. Then his excuse to himself as well as to that boy (whose dignity he would never forget) had been an unfamiliarity with a world where energies throbbed beneath the surface of life, and with those who believed and waited for the mundane to be transformed into the quickened. Then he had been a neophyte. But now? What excuse? Michael had gone out alone onto the firth and returned with a girl wrapped only in his greatcoat. Surely Robert's silence was as cutting now as his words had been years before.

What had he said her name was? Aude. She had stood there, sensual, ephemeral, yet at the same time not at all out of place in this homely, solid kitchen. She had begun to speak to him, but he had looked away.

Michael's soft, determined voice interrupted these reveries.

"It's Connla in reverse, Robert. I always believed the

fairy maiden should have stayed. And now she has arrived.''

He turned a face still flushed, eyes feverishly bright.

"She's here. Aude is upstairs. Finally.''

Like Connla.

Robert turned and stared into the fire.

Oh, those old, disquieting tales, they weren't a lather to be washed off and forgotten. They sank into the bones, they lay dormant in the marrow, they coursed the blood, to haunt and fret the heart. Like the past!

No, there was too much pure joy in Michael's face for these aging fears. He would put them aside. Aude had come and there was a transformation in Michael as palpable as the one Robert had felt within himself on first contact with that boy of ten standing on the pier. No, he would not dwell on the future, any more than on the past. One could not second-guess life; he'd learned that lesson on a grand scale, writ large.

But there was a question. Olaf was moving about in his house slippers refilling cups, teapot in one hand, milk pitcher in the other.

"Might I ask, Michael Magnus,'' Robert said, shaking his head at Olaf's offer of milk, "has the girl told you anything of her home, her family?'' *Why am I asking? How unctuous I sound!*

Olaf shuffled in place, making a rather pointless exchange of teapot and pitcher on the sideboard.

Moments passed until the answer came.

"I've told you where she's from, Robert.''

The fire gave a low sputter.

"And I know where all should be goin'.'' Olaf moved in

quickly to fill the painful silence. Leaning toward the fire, he held out his pocket watch. "Hour's goin' on ten. Finish up the tea, both o' ye, and we'll find Anny. I'll warrant she's put Aude firm in bed."

Michael pushed up on his heels, the teacup rattling in his hand. The laird nodded to Olaf as he walked briskly from the room. A moment later the other two followed.

They came on Michael and Anny by the front stairway. The full arc of Anny's bosom swelled as she announced triumphantly:

"She's asleep, poor lamb. Gone before I could give her the grog. Said she'd come from far, she had. I've tucked her in proper. She won't stir the night."

Olaf was already a few stairs up.

"I'll leave a light burnin' in the hallway," he said. "It won't do, havin' her wanderin' in the dark should she be wakin' and not rememberin' where she be. Comin', Master Robin?"

Chapter Nineteen _____

TEACUPS, TEAPOT, SAUCERS lay draining by the tin wash-basin. Murphy had not stirred, the fire was a bed of glowing peat chunks. Anny looked up from her perch on the stool as Olaf came in.

"Ye took *her* clothes for the girl, eh?" The old skipper settled onto his usual stool. "'Twasn't easy, I'll warrant."

"It near killed me, openin' up that trunk. But I had to, didn't I? She'll be needin' clothes and the laddie's so far gone with love he'll not be askin' where an' all. How'd ye know?" The woman suddenly realized she'd not said, beforehand or after, what she'd done.

Olaf chuckled.

"I'll say it again, if I've not said it a million times. We've not lived side by side these many years fur me not to know yur mind, Anny Anderson. It be clear the child's nothin' on beneath, and where were the garments to come from? Besides, I took one look at yur face by the stairs. Try as ye might, I know ye!" He looked around. "It's spankin' clean here; ye could o' waited."

"'Tween't a thing to do, a few cups and all. Will ye have a last one?"

165

A few minutes later the final ritual of the evening was under way.

"Ye'll never use the cup, will ye?" Olaf grinned as Anny filled her saucer for the second time.

"Enough 'round here'll be changin', never mind how I drink my tea. Olaf, what do ye make o' it all?"

Olaf didn't answer immediately; his eyes flickered.

"Well, she's . . . she's a feast, I'd say, and that's not what ye're askin', is it?"

Anny put down the saucer.

"Ye know what I'm askin'. Ye saw the laddie's face. What do ye say to it?"

"I'd say he's past rescuin' and if he's anythin' like his father, he'll not be comin' near such a one again."

"And the girl? Aude? Straight now. It's not her looks I'm enquirin' after. Even I can see them. No, I'm askin' . . ."

"Is she past rescuin', too, is what ye want to know? I'd say aye, though it's harder to know with a woman." Olaf got up and came around to Anny, putting a hand on her arm. "But from my little knowin', we've naught to fear. She's a strong'n, she is. The life fairly jumps from her, and that's what he be needin', Michael Magnus. She's a lot like her, ye're thinkin', eh, Anny?" And with the mention of the Lady Lavinia, Anny folded her hands over his.

"*There,* ye see! Ye be feelin' it, too!"

Olaf gave her a puzzled look.

"Feelin' what? What is it I be feelin', Anny Anderson?"

"Ye been watchin' the firth, same as me. Watchin' the laddie, morn till night, day in, day out. And home he comes with her. Where'd ye think she's from, have ye asked yurself, Olaf Haroldson? Have ye?"

"Ah, that. Well now, it's strange ye come to it, fur Master Robin was askin' the laddie just that a while ago."

Now Anny's eyes flickered.

"Did he now? And what be the answer?"

"'I told you where she's from, Robert,' was what he said. Laird to his toes," Olaf added with open pride.

"Then it's from the firth she's come and that's that." And Anny repeated the words as if to a child. "It's from the firth she's come, and you know it, Olaf Haroldson."

"It's crossed yur mind there'll be a weddin'?"

"Aye."

"And how'll it sound to the minister—'She's from the firth, and that's that'? He be no fool."

"He's no fool but he's no neighbor, neither. We'll have the one from Lerwick, and for him the child's from Burrafirth, left an orphan, always been called Aude."

As he listened, it was clear Anny's solution was a comfort to herself alone, for the incredulity on Olaf's part quickly turned to worry. She was not that far into her own plans to miss the change.

"Don't ye see?" Anny had certainly not grown less insistent with age. Olaf set his pipe by the cup. "It don't matter to any o' us where she's from. She's *here,* and somewhere out *there* it was writ. Before God she's his wife, whatever the minister puts down. Ye know it, I know it, and so does Robin, though I'm thinkin' it's hardest fur him—but he'll come 'round. I been thinkin' it's time he were goin' south, but that's another thing. . . . I'm not sayin' we'll not have the rites neat and proper. I'm only sayin' we don't have to say more'n we have to say."

"Ye're a crafty old herring trader, Anny! No, ye're

right.'' With his thumb Olaf pushed a tobacco plug deep into the pipe's bowl. ''We've no need to speak more'n we're asked. We've lived up here, a peerie family, and the crofters and fisherfolk have a good life with us, to be sure. It's no business o' anyone's exceptin' ours. When ye get down to it,'' he said, taking his long thin stick, catching a flame, and lighting the pipe, ''when it's all said, it be only their business. We'll be touched by 'em, that's fur sure, by those two, if we've not been already.'' And their gazes met across the table.

Robert snuffed out the candle.

He'd leave on his hose. It was bitter cold, though the fire in the grate had been roasting all evening. In the trapped warmth of the bed his body gave up some of its tautness, and so did his heart.

Which philosopher had written that we meet ourselves again and again, or—in another sense—that we never come to someone or something on completely new ground? Always there is a harking back to a terrain we thought the wild grasses had taken over, or the impenetrable shrub or the brambled wood without path. But there is no such place.

Where was the bright-faced girl with the wide laughing mouth and hair like broom against whose love he had sought out the farthest isle of the realm as refuge? This was the desolate revelation, in its full implication, like a negative epiphany, that had entered him as Aude had entered the kitchen: his flight had been from himself and not from Isobel. Was it now to be a double loss? Was he losing Michael as well? If five years ago were today, what . . .

He raised up and fumbled with the pillow, turning it over.

It was wet and his face was wet. And he was beset by a loneliness he had counted on never knowing again.

The birds were making early-morning noises. A light diffused the walls. Someone had started up a fire.

Aude's hand found the clothes. Stockings. Up and over the knees as far as they would go. Shift. Over the head. She shook herself and the petticoat dropped below her ankles. She rolled it up at her waist. Dress. Also over the head. The slim tubes of cloth on each side were sleeves. Her arms found their way through and she stared as her hands emerged.

Shoeless she moved, again on tiptoe, along the silent corridor, down the stairs, and through the front door.

Once outside she darted away from the house, hair and skirt streaming behind her. Only when she reached the spot high on the moor where Michael and Robert had once stood watching the haze did she stop.

It was there. A silver mesh of light.

Aude dropped to her knees and leaned over the ledge. The cliff angled out and down, ledge by ledge. At the very bottom a flat of land covered with moss, a greensward, pancaked out into the sea. She remained in that position for several minutes. The haze undulated toward the tiny peninsula, drew in as if to materialize, and a high sweet note sang out from its center. Then it was gone.

Aude breathed a sigh of relief. When she got up, she was smiling. Below, hidden, hanging on a broad jut of ledge, Thomas Matheson saw the haze and heard the sigh.

Two weeks later the minister came to Unst. Snow was

falling the night of his arrival, and in the morning land, water, and sky vied with each other—crystal blue, crystal pink.

Days before Anny had again opened the chest, taking out an oval box worked in silver and enamel and set with irregular gemstones. It was the jewel box belonging to Michael's parents. She removed a man's gold wedding band and its twin, less wide, much smaller in diameter, and—the sight was like a knife to the heart—far less worn. There was no need to try them on. They would fit. Anny polished them halo bright, along with two gold hair torques for Aude's curls. Anny herself had taken them from Lady Lavinia's hair.

And so it was recorded in the library that Michael Magnus, laird of Burrafirth, was married to Mistress Aude, also of Burrafirth, on this day of November in the year 1769, the witnesses being Olaf Haroldson, Robert John, Anny Anderson, and the Reverend William Edwardson.

Aude had told the minister at breakfast that her family was near but could not come. Anny had told him she was orphaned at birth. Chewing slowly on a piece of Anny's choice smoked herring, he had raised a pair of extraordinarily bushy brows, peered at the girl, saw there something whereof he could not speak, swallowed hard, coughed twice, and asked for another cup of tea!

After the signing, there was a table laden with the cellar's best port for all who came to wish them joy. And all came. Block after block of peat went onto the fire, glasses were filled and touched and filled again until well after midnight. Aglow with wine and good wishes and goodwill, the population of Burrafirth departed in small groups.

Just before taking Michael's hand at the bottom of the stairs, Aude turned to Robert.

"We've not had a chance to talk yet, have we?"

And with a smile at once eager and diffident, Aude kissed his cheek.

"Go to her, Robert. Go to Isobel."

In the great canopied bed Aude lay against Michael's chest, his left arm curving around her head, his hand lightly on her shoulder. Husband and wife for only a few hours, they slept now, legs entwined, body to body, heart to heart, their youthful energies spent, but only till they woke to find each other again.

Chapter Twenty _____

Winter
Burrafirth

Alexander the Great,

I have had enough of Myself! Laurence Magnus is
dead. Michael found Oxford no challenge, most of his
peers mental slovens and spiritual vacants; he returned
to us in the Summer.

He is married, Alexander. Her name is Aude, she
emerged from out of the firth. Yes, *I* say this. And she
knows. Knows what, you ask? Before answering,
please note that I have said I have had enough of
Myself; not of Unst, nor Burrafirth, nor the Ness; not
of my little family. No, I place my revulsion where it
belongs. *Finalement*, you exclaim! At least this has
come about, you add. Could it not be, you comment
further to yourself, *sotto voce*, that Robert will *act* on
the disruption of the "order of things"? After all, he is
thirty, his former pupil is sixteen. A man barely past
childhood has bound himself for a life to a creature
from Nowhere. Bound himself in utter joy and *trust*. I
can attest to this. Yet our *so* prudent scholar cannot

take one step forward, though the fair Isobel, whom he has tasted, smelt, taken in his arms, who has openly declared her desire to cast in her lot with his, is clearly from Somewhere, a reality, a creature of flesh and blood.

This is what she knows, Alexander. I tell you, if the Greek Oracles were to show the ancients their true face, they would not be unlike Aude's.

She has already exhorted me to go to Isobel, find her, take her. How much more urging do I need? Michael has been convinced since he was a toddler that his firth was the repository of things wondrous. And from it has come this creature.

I am miserable!
Robert

Late Winter
Aberdeen

Felicitations!

I have a presentiment in my bones! This creature, as you call her, is about to effect the Miraculous. *Lentement;* slowly, of course. O now not so prudent scholar, slowly but inexorably you *are* being moved towards the inevitable. Are you aware of this? I think you are.

Autre theme. Do you recall a *Book of Proverbes* by one John Heywood, circa 1546? The first such collection of English colloquial sayings. I have been dipping into same and have extracted morsels for your now more discerning emotional palate—quite an image, this!

Heywood	*Alexander*
Look ere ye leape.	Ye have looked long enough!
He that will not when he may When he would he shall have Nay	Ergo, Leape, Man, Leape!
When the sun shineth make hay When the iron is hot, strike	Gads, your Iron must be nearly Consumed!
The tide tarrieth no man!	You cannot *count* on the fair Isobel *flowing* for a clod like you have been, forever. But right now she is flowing for you, old cock, she is!
A hard beginning maketh a good ending!	So Up with you, and into her!
Nothing is impossible to a willing Hart.	

Ah! Hart for Heart. Here give me the pleasure of recalling to you one of our favorite passages from the *Shir Ha-Shirim, The Song of Songs:*

My beloved is like a gazelle or a young hart.
I adjure you, O daughters of Jerusalem,
By the gazelles, and by the hinds of the field,
That ye awaken not, nor stir up love
Until it please!

It pleases now, Robert, it *pleases,* which is why I
am awakening hopefully your love for Isobel. No, you
are not free of this Sunday School Missive! Here is
one of which you yourself are a prime example:
"Children learn to creepe ere they can learn to go."
Alors! Go then, God's breath, *go!*
And *finalement,* as you so rightly say I say, I cannot
resist closing but thusly:

Hast thou a friend,
As heart may wish at will?
Then *use him so,*
To have his friendship still.

Perhaps all this will light a fire under your *derrière!*
Plus the following news. I have met the *one.* Yes,
directed to her by your Isobel, whom I suspect led me
thither to be rid of me herself. I must tell you, cock
Robin, we do suit in many ways, we do.

I await from you— Damn it! You know full well
what I await!

Mes Amitiés
Alexandros

P.S. For your tombstone (if you don't get on with it!):

Here lies Robert John
Beaten with his own rod!

You take my meaning?

P.P.S. *Trust* is the key. And the rub for you. You trusted the wrong person. You trusted the reaction of the Beast and not the Beauty. You put all your faith in his ability to ruin your life and none in Isobel's to enhance, nay, to *create*, yours. Magic indeed!

P.P.P.S. Has the sky not been aflame?

"Times ye don't know ye be broodin', Olaf, it gets to be every day o' the life, like. Only when it's turned 'round and ye wake up smilin', then ye say, Aye! We've been broodin', all o' us. Aye!"

Anny and Olaf were folding linen on the front turf. It was mid-April and the sun, unusually warm, had bleached the sheets as white as an ivory gull.

Five months had passed since Aude had walked in through the kitchen door hand in hand with Michael.

"Hear, Olaf!" Anny looked up. In the sky a lark, as if picking up their joy, was filling the air with sheer delight.

"Hear that? Why, he's been pourin' out his tiny heart like that forever and where've I been? Where've ye been? Not hearin' him like we're hearin' him today, I'll tell ye."

Olaf came up to Anny with his end of a large hand-embroidered sheet, joining it to hers.

"Aye, we've all been turned 'round, Anny Anderson. Like ye been remarkin' to Robin, she's got to be grand inside as out. Like ye were feelin' the first time ye saw him.

When I took 'em to the graves, ye should have seen her face. All a mix o' smiles and tears and repeatin' again and again, It's all right now, it's all right. And Michael Magnus standin' there proud and tall as the mast o' the *Erne,* he was. If I'd a net I'd've caught the love, so thick it was. Then he put the gold torques in her hair, right there, in front o' them, o' the laird and the lady. Then he said—"

Anny broke in, "And what did *she* say when she saw 'em, Olaf?" She tried to toss off the question as she tossed stale bread to Swaabie and the other birds, but to Olaf's ear there was a quality behind it that was far from casual.

"It's like ye to ask. She gave an answer that's pullin' in me, Anny, she did. The laddie took 'em from the box, the one all velvet lined, and put 'em in her hair. 'I wanted to give them to you *here,*' he said, then he kissed the top o' her head like he does." And the two smiled on a scene that repeated itself day in and day out through the day. Olaf raised a finger. "Then the young laird said, 'They were my mother's.' Quiet-like, he said it."

"And?" Anny was holding her breath.

" '*I know,*' the mistress answered. "Aye, she did and I'm still shook up. But not those two, not at all they weren't. The mistress put down the flowers on the two graves and got up smilin' and we left. Well?" Olaf added a smoothed folded sheet to the pile on the stone wall and waited.

"Well?" Anny was shaking a pillowcase rather more violently than necessary. "It's all part o' what's happenin'. It's *there,* fur all o' us. Even fur Robin lad, I'll tell ye, Olaf Haroldson, that Robin's a field readyin' fur plantin'. There's a churnin' and a swellin', Olaf, and a painin' about him. Aye, it's the painin' tells me he's readyin'. Ye been noticin'?"

"Aye, he's been painin'. He's no skylark these days, nor whistlin' like he used to do. Here we are happier'n ever and that lad goes 'round about like he's lost all."

"Emptyin' out to be filled, that's it. He's gettin' ready, he is."

"Gettin' ready?"

"Aye, that's what I said, gettin' ready. Have ye forgotten the Lady Isobel?"

Olaf took out his pipe, his "thinkin' tool," he used to call it when Michael, as a child, would then beg for a puff.

Before he could answer, Anny gave Murphy a brisk nudge off a pale-blue silk shift that had slipped to the ground. "That dog'll go one too much."

Murphy's tail wagged agreeably.

"Men!" She laid the shift lovingly over her arm and pointed to the linen. "Aye, the Lady Isobel. Plain as that pipe o' yurs, he's stirrin' to somethin'. Kindly take up that linen, Olaf. Least that's big and plain enough fur ye to see. By the way, have ye noticed anythin' different about?"

"Only that Thomas Matheson be too often skulkin' by the back kitchen gardens or floatin' along in that wreck of a boat o' his, too close to the Ness fur my comfort."

Anny stopped, a red flush appearing in streaks along her neck and hairline.

"*Lord,* Olaf, have a talk with him. See if ye can gentle him along. Or better still, spirit him away. These be not the days fur the likes o' him about."

"That one be trouble any day o' the week, Anny. Strange it is—these last years since the mornin' Michael fair cursed him out, he's stopped the stranglin'; but me, instead o' bein' pleased like was the laird, I'm up nights wonderin' what Thomas is gettin' ready to do. I'll have to be speakin' to him, but first to the young laird. But there's more meanin' in your words, Anny.''

"Lord, aye, Olaf Haroldson, you wouldn't miss it in a sheep! The mistress! She's makin' a baby. It's begun these four months, and she bein' so slim an' all, but it's there, fur sure it is!''

Michael put his head on Aude's stomach. They were lying naked on the bed.

"He's very busy tonight, my love.''

Michael kissed Aude's navel, then each breast. They were swelling deliciously, he thought, and the nipples were like pink pearls set on widening rounds of tortoiseshell, firm and yielding to his mouth.

Aude looked at her husband. His smile disarmed her, it would always disarm her, and his touch turned her bones to water.

Michael's hand covered the triangle of tight black curls, then moved along her groin, his fingers flattening out as he came closer to the moist cave's entrance to her body.

Aude rolled on her side into his embrace. Michael bit the tip of her nose, then rubbed his teeth against a knuckle. Her hands were fragrant. He felt the love gathering in her limbs and in his loins.

In the fullness of its parents' love the child turned and stirred. From one end of its watery home to the other it shivered under the taut skin, then dropped away back into its cradle of flesh. Only when the two slept in the fulfillment of love did the child within the womb sleep its own sleep, dreaming, perhaps, of its own fulfillment.

Chapter Twenty-one _____

"THE WORLD BE wick this mornin', mistress." Anny tied Aude's skirt lightly around her burgeoning waist. "And so be that baby in ye." She grinned, then, unable to contain her pride, she stood away appraising and approving what she saw. "Oh, mistress, we *all* be wick since ye come. Ye know how long it's been since there was another woman in this house? 'Tis a lonely place, though there be those thinkin', 'Oh, Anny Anderson, she's her own way these years.' 'Tis not so, Mistress Aude. 'Tis been a lonely place."

Aude took Anny's hands, arms stretched out by her side. They stood smiling, two children ready to swing.

"Anny, waiting is a lonely vigil. He's beautiful, isn't he?" And she blushed in the exuberance of her fifteen years.

"Aye, beautiful, but he be a stubborn one when he's a mind fur it. Ye've not seen it yet?"

"Not yet, but I will, I'm sure, and I'm sure I shan't mind. He can't be perfect, can he? Otherwise what will we all do before such a paragon?"

"A what?"

"A paragon. It means a thing or person of superior quality."

"Well, well, Michael Magnus, he be that and I'm findin' ye be as full o' learnin' as he. What'll I do with the pair o' ye, talkin' such words. Where—"

The blush intensified. Anny saw it and a hand flew to her cheek.

"Mistress! I'm not askin', nor will I, I shan't. I know—"

"Anny, it's all right." She paused. "Do you know what I'd really like to do this morning? I'd like to go 'round to the kitchen gardens and see what's coming up, and we can make plans and you can show me how to plant. You must show me *everything*, Anny, now that spring has come!"

The grin was back.

"Aye, I'll be showin' ye and I'll be aidin' ye when yur time comes. End o' August, is it?"

"End of August. But we don't have to make any plans about that. . . . Not yet," she added tentatively. "Let's go! Do you know, Swaabie never lets me out of his sight. Black-backed gulls are like that, protectors, aren't they? Of—"

"O' the seals, special-like. He be warnin' the seals when the hunters be nearby." And Anny found her heart bumping along like a broken wagon wheel. Suddenly she had no breath.

"We should go out now." Aude picked up her shawl from the trunk.

"The air was full of smells last night, spring smells, Anny!" She peered at the old nurse, whose face had gone ashen. "Anny, it's all right. Please, Anny. It's a wick day and we're all wick, like you say, and I've Michael's child in my womb. Isn't that a glory, Anny, a glory! Come on!''

The three men had assembled in the library.

"I'd completely forgotten it," Michael was saying to Olaf and Robert. "Months ago I encountered Anny's grand-nephew Edward at the boathouse. He was fretting terri-bly''—he hesitated—''over something he'd seen on the firth, from Suther's Fields. He said Thomas Matheson had seen it also, obviously meaning that he was there or near; he added that something glittered in his hand, which could mean a knife, could it not?'' Michael drew spread fingers through his hair.

"I'm not sure I understand." Robert was tired. He had just returned from Baltasound where he had business with David Gifford, laird of Balta, a lifelong friend of Laurence, now old and ailing, without heirs. The meeting had raised nagging doubts about Robert's future, for the laird had asked—either in all innocence or all shrewdness—what his plans were now that Michael Magnus was back and wed-ded. Somewhere between Balta and the Ness it had oc-curred to him that the old laird may well have been sounding him out in order to offer him a position. By the time he was asked by Olaf to join them in the library the pain of conflict, to stay, or to go and find Isobel, had reached a new intensity.

"Robert," Olaf answered quickly, "what I've been dis-cussin' these days with the young laird be the followin'. Thomas Matheson be lurkin' these last years, we know this. Times he works fur me, times he disappears, times he lurks. Since that day Michael Magnus here gave him a piece o' his mind, there's been little stranglin' o' birds, but Anny 'n' me, we're uneasy in our hearts, what with the mistress floatin' about and the babby comin', and now, what Michael just be reportin', though it's five months ago. I wish . . .''

"That he'd been exiled years ago?" Robert pushed up in the chair, warming to the gravity of the problem.

"Aye, that Master Laurence had put him off the island into a place fur them that's mad, fur sure he's his mad times, but that don't make him less feared, though yur father, bless his soul, he was forgivin' him fur that, and trustin'. No, he were wrong to trust. That Thomas, he be sly enough along with it and he be understandin' when he wants somethin'. I've worked with him. I've known him all my life. He's a mix, is Thomas.''

Robert turned to Michael. "It's not too late, is it, to act?"

Michael smiled at his friend.

"Aude would say it's never too late to act. But seriously, my father came to me that night after my outburst and warned me that Thomas Matheson has a memory like a trap. I'd forgotten that, also. It all comes back. The question now is exactly the one you've posed. What's to be done? We are now responsible for the others, for all on the estate. Olaf?''

"Fur sure we are, young laird. And I can give you Anny's amen on that. You should have seen her last night, the flush in that old face when I put my worries to her. Aye, ye've her amen to that.''

"What do you suggest?''

"Well, he's right now in his disappearin' time. I'll go up to the cottage sniffin' a bit.''

"I'll go with you." Robert stood up and buttoned his vest. "Now?"

"Good a time as any." Olaf opened the door. "By the way, Michael Magnus, if ye be missin' Swaabie a' times, he's takin' to walkin' up the heels o' the mistress. He's near as good a companion as Murphy. Got more brains, to my mind."

This was an old saw between them, from the time Swaabie and Murphy had entered the family, and they thoroughly enjoyed sparring over it. Michael laughed.

"We should set up a wager after all these years, which is the most efficient protector."

Later, remembering this exchange, Robert also recalled that a strange look had come into Olaf's eyes, but it was fleeting and gone before the three left the room.

Thomas Matheson's cottage was a miserable, clay-floored, windowless, chimneyless cabin. One hundred years before all the cottages of Burrafirth had been rebuilt from what could have been called hovels to decent, chimneyed, relatively airy living establishments. Thomas's grandfather had resisted the modernization. Olaf related this information as he and Robert opened the slatted door of the byre and walked into the main cottage.

They were stopped by the nauseating acrid smell of decayed and decaying flesh. Up to the ceiling, with hardly a corridor between, had been piled layer upon layer of dead rabbits slit from the gullet to the anus, some with eyes bulging, others gauged out. There hung in the air a ghastly silence. The horror froze their bodies, forced them to survey what their wildest imaginings—and each had fancied some bizarre discovery—had not even skirted. They pulled their scarves up over their noses and each waited for the other to proceed toward the but and ben of the cottage.

There, an even more horrific scene confronted them. Thomas had an old cow and an old pony. Both lay stiff in their blood, congealed and black. Both had been strangled with a length of rope; then their heads had been tied together so that their bodies formed a V and in its crotch was a bouquet of powdering meadowsweet.

There was no sign of life. The few chickens Thomas kept had fled the massacre or had themselves been mangled and thrown God knows where. Robert noted the cobwebs strung across a food cupboard were unbroken.

"The Devil took hold o' him!" Olaf was no longer the composed stalwart Viking standing fast by his longship; he was seething and under his breath he added, "May the Devil *take* him!"

Robert's tongue was dust in his mouth and his hands were wet with a cold sweat.

"He's gone, Olaf."

"Lord save us from his return!"

"We'll have to get all of this out of here."

Olaf pulled Robert toward the door.

"Ivar. Ivar's the man fur it. Close-mouthed, understandin'. Always said Thomas should be put away. He'll not scare the others on the land. He'll do it right and quiet."

They made a pact. They would not say a word to Anny. They would tell Michael that there was no sign of Thomas and that it appeared he had been gone some time. And they two would keep out a weather eye. That was all.

"There it be, mistress. Ye'll be havin' a fill o' berries— three, four kinds—and greens galore. That babby'll be fat and sassy 'fore it gets here! Are ye or the laddie minded, be it a boy child or a girl child?''

Aude arched her back, exaggerating the roundness of her stomach.

''Strong and healthy is what we want. I suppose we have to think about names. Have you any ideas, Anny?'' Then she laughed, answering her own question. ''You've always ideas!''

''Aye, I do—and right now, I've an idea I'd like to be puttin' a molucca bean 'round your neck. Could I be doin' this, mistress?''

Aude pirouetted toward the kitchen door.

''Don't you think love will protect me, Anny?'' Then, seeing the crestfallen look: ''Yes, you may. *Certainly*, Anny.''

In the cubicle by the kitchen, her room, Anny pulled a straw box from under her bed. She had prepared the necklace the night before, after hours of anguished tossing. She had strung the bean on a black wresting thread, knotted like the one she had twined around Michael's broken arm when he was a child.

Aude sat on the end of the bed.

''Why are there nine knots?''

''Because it takes nine knots fur the charm to work, child.''

''That's a fine straight answer!''

Aude turned slightly and lowered her head. Anny waved the necklace in the air, chanting softly.

'' 'The Lord rade and the foal slade; He lighted and He righted. Set joint to joint, bone to bone, healin' the Holy Ghost's name.' ''

Aude looked up.

"But Anny, I've broken nothing."

Anny tied the thread nine times on Aude's neck.

"'Tis the charm fur bone or sinew. I'm thinkin', the way ye be scramblin' about this land, 'tis best put all the power behind ye, fur the good. Aye." She placed a hand on the top of Aude's hair and shut her eyes. "Aye, there be no harm in it and a power o' good, a power o' good."

Chapter Twenty-two _____

AUDE WENT SERENELY about the house and land. Robert and Olaf hid their anxiety in work or short expeditions, but they were never away more than a few hours, and never away at the same time. Michael was barely able to contain his pride and eagerness as the baby swelled within the womb. Anny watched the molucca bean.

On a hot, dry August morning Michael and Aude sat in the lee of a cornfield waiting for the corncrake to show itself. Purple and muted green, the tufted vetch twined among the stalks. Bees slooped lazily searching out the pads of kidney vetch and the tall hardy cornsow thistle.

A slight crackling and a pair of baby crakes emerged from the far end of the field.

"Oh, my love, they're very, very rarely seen. Anny would surely say it's luck!"

Aude puckered up her mouth. "She laments, sir, her husband goes this morning abirding!"

"But with his wife and child, sir, so be merry, girl!" Michael crawled away on all fours to the end of the low barrow against which they were resting. A few minutes later, as the chicks were obviously not threatened by his presence, he turned to wave Aude closer. She was gone.

Scrambling to his feet, he raced back to the stubble path down which they'd come, calling out, then, in panic, screaming her name.

Around a curve he saw her. She seemed to float on the air—she was being pulled, he realized, and his panic increased. He could not catch up. He must at least keep her in sight.

He saw her come to the very edge of the cliff, saw her put one foot over the side—and disappear. A moment later he heard her scream.

Gaining the same crest, Michael paused for breath. Looking down, he saw what he thought at first was a string of kelp dangling from a sharp jut of rock. It was Aude's necklace. Michael drew back from the drop, dizzy and nauseated. The molucca bean was black.

"She wasn't wearing it. I would have seen it! *Aude!*"

Aude was stretched out below on a round of turf, a carpet of seapinks. Tiny whitecaps formed a water garland around the hoop of land. Legs apart, she was as naked as the day she had climbed into his boat. A spurt of bright-red blood came from her side, falling over her belly like a fountain. The knife was still in her.

"God in Heaven!"

Michael slid down the side like a piece of scree breaking off the cliff and bouncing to the water, the ragged surface slashing into his palms.

He reached her side, reached to pull the knife from her flesh. A thin silver mesh struck his hand and he fell back. A brilliant light blinded him. When he opened his eyes the turf lay bare.

Dazed with horror Michael cushioned his head in the spot

where a moment before Aude had lain. Looking out over the water, he saw no sign of either the light or the girl.

Anny, Olaf, and Robert clustered over Swaabie's limp form.

"It's the doin' o' that Thomas Matheson. But how's he come near and us not seein' him fur months now, Olaf? With us watchin'? How?"

Olaf looked at Robert, but before either could venture an answer Michael fell into their circle, his face awash with sweat and tears, his hair plastered against his head.

"Laddie! What's taken ye?" Anny held out her arms as he collapsed against her. Then he saw the dead gull.

"It's him, then, it's got to be him. I tried to pull out the knife but the lightning stopped me. I—"

"Where is Aude, Michael Magnus? What knife, where were you? Please, laddie, *get it out*. What happened?" And Olaf was shaking his young master, for it was clear that the worst had happened.

Michael stretched toward the gull.

"Swaabie, Swaabie, you could have saved her. You would have warned me. . . ." He turned to Anny, his face seared with anguish. "The molucca bean, Anny; it turned black. But she wasn't wearing it. I didn't see it till . . . She must have had it in her pocket. . . ."

"Young laird, Michael Magnus, tell us where Aude is." Robert cupped his hand firmly under Michael's chin. "Do you hear me? You want her saved, tell us where this happened."

"By the hoop of turf, the greensward below the large puffin colony. But she's not there anymore, she's—"

"I'll get a rope and we'll take two boats. It's not that far and is best approached by the water. Ivar will—"

Anny shot out an arm, her mouth moving silently, her eyes closed.

"Ye'll have to be findin' Thomas Matheson or ye'll not be savin' her." She stared at Olaf, her eyes popping. "Aye, fur it'll be the magic o' sympathy doin' the savin', and 'tis only Thomas Matheson able to pull that knife fur all it be his. That were the cause o' the lightnin'. Get Thomas Matheson and go after her, God save us all!"

Michael grabbed Anny's skirt.

"Anny, we can't go after her. She's drowned, she was pulled . . . oh, God, I think she was pulled into the water. She's—"

"Can't go after her, laddie? What be *ye* sayin' to Anny— ye, who be the young laird o' Burrafirth? What be yur life if not fur goin' after her? Do ye suddenly have to *see* to be actin'?"

It took no more. Michael took a deep breath, and the old command was back in his stance and in his voice.

"Anny, do you think you could get down the incline?"

The answer in her eyes was an unqualified aye.

"Then Olaf will muster Ivar with a rope and boat. Robert?"

"I'm with you to Matheson's cottage, young laird. I'm with you."

Thomas Matheson was standing by the stoop, the sheath of a sealing knife in his hand. Waiting. His cap was pulled down over his eyes and a thin long beard straggled out from under his scarf. Without a word Michael took one arm, Robert the other, and they swept him down to the boathouse and into a rowboat, the very one in which Michael had spent his days scouring the firth. Thomas offered no resistance.

Olaf was already racing along the water. He could spot Anny easing her way cautiously along a pencil-thin path that wandered down, a much longer but much safer route for one of her bulk.

In the second boat Thomas shook off Robert's grip and kept his eyes lowered. Michael took up the oars and began rowing furiously.

"You're coming down under the water with me, Thomas Matheson. We're going to find my wife and you will extract your knife from her side."

This said with an infinite calm. Robert sat marveling at the transformation, for there was no reason to assume that Aude would be alive when, and if, they found her. Yet for Michael there was no doubt.

The water around the greensward was still. As Olaf let his boat drift toward the hoop, Michael threw off his knitted tunic and pulled off his boots. His dive cut the water like an arrow. A gull dipped and flew off with its wriggling prey.

Anny was on her knees at the edge of the turf. Now the two boats were side by side.

"Oh, Lord, she's prayin'." Olaf's boat banged against the other. *"What have ye done, Thomas Matheson? What have ye done?!"*

The silence held. Robert, Anny, Olaf, and even Thomas were looking to the circlet where Michael entered the water.

What seemed eternity passed and passed again.

"How long can he stay under?"

"Ye been with him in the water, Master Robin. Aye, but not under it, that's true. Longer'n most, longer. . . ."

A hand came over the corner of Olaf's boat and Michael's head emerged. If he had seen death or nothing, both were in his eyes.

"Nothing! There's not a sign of her. *Not a sign!*"

On land Anny rose to her feet, arms outstretched, hands clasped together.

"God be thanked. *God be thanked!*"

They looked at Anny, and in a split second Thomas was over the side of the boat, and down, a mass of bubbles marking the spot.

In as fast a time Michael swam around the boat, curled over and down, and reemerged with Thomas. Pulling him, he came up to Olaf's side.

"Take him in your boat, Olaf. He'll not get away again, nor be redeemed so easily. Oh, no, not he!"

"Oh, no, not he. Well, where she be?" It was the same grotesque, contorted face Olaf remembered from that fatal morning, *the cause of it all.* Just this once he allowed himself the utterly useless thought, but once only, for it had happened and could not be called back. So many things. . . .

"Feelin' an' reelin', Old Tom went asealin', Old Tom. . . ."

Michael bellowed, "That's *it! Anny!*"

Whether or not Anny heard Thomas's prattle, she was furiously waving her left arm toward the end of the firth, then arcing it. Pointing and arcing it.

"I know, Anny. I know. That's the place we'll find her. By the seals! I'm sure of it. You're right, God be thanked. They took her there."

Michael was climbing impatiently into the boat, fairly pushing Robert to the bottom while he himself took up the oars again.

"We're off, Anny! Mother told me the seals guard the magic. Aude is magic, we all know that. Robert, Olaf! Aude is my magic and the seals have surely saved her. Now you'll see, Thomas Matheson, you'll witness something you've never conjured up in that confused head of yours. You'll see!"

There was only one thought in the minds of Olaf and Robert. The last human being found among the seals had been the Lady Lavinia—and she had not been saved.

Anny was back down on her knees.

"Lord, don't let it happen again. Oh, Master Laurie, the laddie mustn't have to live it as ye did. And ye died a broken heart. Oh, Lord! Why so much fur us poor creatures?" Then a thought came into her mind that seemed to gather strength. "Work with the magic, Lord. *This time,* help the mistress."

They rounded the headland. Michael rowed close to the rock, which was bare of seals.

"Olaf!" he called to the skipper, who was rowing up behind him. "Keep a hand on Thomas. I'm going down. I'll find Aude and I'll bring her up. I've changed my mind. I don't trust Thomas Matheson, to take him down with me. He's likely to get away or . . ."

"Or drown." Robert began shedding his boots and tunic. "I'm coming with you, Michael Magnus."

"You *can't!* Robert! You've no experience at this. It's not easy."

"Easy or no, I'm coming. Please, Michael, for once in my life let me *do* something. It will be all right. I know it." He smiled. "I'm with you."

The look on Michael's face was of understanding and gratitude.

Olaf secured his boat to Michael's. Thomas sat motionless, eyes wild.

Robert and Michael floated downward, Michael's hair streaming behind him. At first they both experienced a terrifying pressure in their lungs, but as they neared the bottom it seemed to let up and suddenly they were breathing normally, their vision filled with minute air bubbles.

They came up against a hedge of shimmering green and silver fronds growing out of the seabed. Waving and undulating, the plants separated as they approached and they flowed through the entrance.

Everywhere there were seals. Lolling or sleeping, skidding along the sand floor one after the other or in pairs, cavorting and sporting. Michael scanned the mass of activity. Aude was not there.

Then he noticed in the far corner what seemed like a huge pile of grey fur. As he and Robert approached, the pile fell away. Aude lay beneath, eyes closed, her legs drawn up against her belly. The knife was in her side. There was no blood.

In an instant they were beside her. Motioning to Robert, Michael took up her head and shoulders, while Robert held firmly to her ankles. The seals watched, but did not try to stop them.

With short, powerful kicks they forced their way to the surface.

Olaf was seated beside Thomas. Seeing Aude, he started up.

"A minute, Olaf, a minute," Michael panted.

Maneuvering so that the side with the knife was accessible, they held Aude against the boat.

"Take it out, Thomas Matheson."

The man huddled further into himself.

"Take his hand and put it on the knife, Olaf. Put it on the knife and make him pull. *Make him pull.*"

Olaf took hold of Thomas's right arm. The man's whole body had gone rigid. Grasping the hand at the wrist, Olaf set it on the knife, holding the fingers against the handle.

"Pull, for God's sake, Thomas, pull. Don't damn yurself more'n ye have already. *Pull!*"

A faint animal cry came from Thomas. His fingers twitched under the pressure of Olaf's hand.

As the knife came away, Olaf released the man's hand. Thomas plunged over the side of the boat and was gone.

And so was the wound in Aude's side.

Michael lifted her high above the water; Olaf took her from him and laid her gently on the bottom of the boat, covering her with Robert's vest.

Mid-August
Burrafirth

Alexander *Felix:*

And that is what happened. The story, that part, is over. A boy and girl were born yesterday, about five minutes apart. The boy has a crescent scar on the bottom of his heel. The girl is perfect.

My little family, augmented thus, is ecstatically happy. Thomas's body was washed up onto that hoop of land; yes, what an irony! But thank goodness for it.

If we had not all seen him dead and gone for sure, we would forever have been wondering where he would turn up.

And your prudent scholar? Well, will you allow me, for once, a poetic gesture toward myself? For truly I entered the water half and reemerged whole. *Tu comprends?*

Whole enough to "go south," as Anny puts it. Yes, I am off next week to Aberdeen, with great hopes and no fears, for it is another Robert John coming to face the tyrant, and face him I will. Yes, I have written to Isobel. Yes. She has waited for me, but will have to wait no longer.

I look forward to our reunion, our weddings, and to a trip into the Arctic where Michael and Aude have invited all of us for an extended vacation—who *knows* what may happen!

Your Robert John, also *Felix!*

COLLECTIONS OF FANTASY AND SCIENCE FICTION

MAGICQUEST

Dear Fantasy Reader,
Ace Books has brought you the best
in adult fantasy for over thirty years.
Now we are pleased to offer the very
best in young adult fantasy, under
our MagicQuest logo. MagicQuest
brings classic and popular works of
YA fantasy into paperback for fantasy
readers and collectors of all ages.

___ 80839-5/$2.25 **THE THROME OF THE ERRIL OF SHERILL**
Patricia A. McKillip

The Throme of Erril of Sherill, a book of songs more beautiful than
the stars themselves does not exist. But if the Cnite Caerles is to
win the sad-eyed daughter of the King of Everywhere, he must find
it, and so he sets out on an impossible quest...
Illustrated by Judith Mitchell. By the World Fantasy Award-winning
author of *The Forgotten Beasts of Eld* and *The Riddle-Master Trilogy*.

___ 65956-X/$2.25 **THE PERILOUS GARD,** *Elizabeth Marie Pope*

Based loosely on the ballad *Tam Lin*, this is the tale of a young man
in bondage to the Queen of the Fairies, and a young woman who
ventures deep into the fairy realms to win him back again...
Newbery Honor Winner and ALA Notable Book.

___ 03115-3/$2.25 **THE ASH STAFF,** *Paul R. Fisher*

Mole is the oldest of six orphans raised by an old sorcerer in the
magical land of Mon Ceth. When their protector dies, Mole must take
up his staff and become the leader of the orphan band. As they
leave the safety of their mountain, little do they know that the are about
to plunge headlong into war. First in the popular *Ash Staff* series.

___ 82630-X/$2.25 **TULKU**, *Peter Dickinson*

Peter Dickinson is best known to fantasy readers for *The Blue Hawk* —
and for *Tulku,* a splendid tale of a young American boy in 19th century
China who travels to the myth-ridden mountains of Tibet — where
the magic is real. An ALA Notable Book.

___ 16621-0/$2.25 **THE DRAGON HOARD**, *Tanith Lee*

Lee has been called "The Princess of Royal Heroic Fantasy" by
The Village Voice — but before she became a bestselling adult writer
Ms. Lee had already made a name for herself with several tales
of YA fantasy adventure. Wacky, wonderful and thoroughly magical,
Ms. Lee's YA fiction is available in paperback for the first time.

Prices may be slightly higher in Canada.